Christmas at
Sleigh Bell Farm

Christmas at Sleigh Bell Farm

An Elliotts of Montana Romance

Kaylie Newell

TULE
PUBLISHING

Chapter One

L UCKY ELLIOTT WASN'T always lucky. Not by a long shot. But that's what folks in town had always called him, and he'd always answered to it. Good-naturedly, of course. Because that was his thing.

But standing there, looking up at the Graff Hotel with the first snowflakes of the season swirling around his head, he wondered if anyone would ever call him by his given name. Or if they'd ever know him well enough to try.

Hunching his shoulders against the chilly Montana breeze, he reached for the door handle and opened it to a blast of warm, fragrant air. The place always smelled like cinnamon and wood smoke. And home. It was his favorite place to grab a beer whenever he came home from college. He hadn't been back in a while, though. Graduate school, or trying to stay *in* graduate school, had overshadowed everything else lately, including stopping in at the Graff, and catching up with his friend who tended bar there.

Lucky looked around the stately old hotel decked out in its holiday finery. Lit wreaths with red velvet bows hung in every frosted window, and a giant blue spruce towered in the lobby beside the spiraling staircase. Silver bells hung from the tree's branches, reflecting the soft light that spilled out from the bar.

A couple of women walked past and gave him flirty smiles. He grinned back, tipping an imaginary hat. One of them laughed and lowered her lashes, reminding him that he still had a firm grip on that part of his life at least. He'd never had a problem with the ladies. So. There was that.

And then his gaze settled on the bulletin board next to the bar entrance. The spot usually reserved for local babysitting services and cattle dog puppies had a new flyer hanging from it. The big wording caught his eye—a contest of some sort. But it was the prize that he immediately zeroed in on. *Winner gets free advertising during the month of December!*

He took a couple steps forward, his cowboy boots thudding on the gleaming wood floor. *It's Support Your Local Business Month in Marietta!* the flyer said. It was framed with little snowmen and clusters of mistletoe. Lucky rubbed his jaw. Somebody was *extremely* excited about Christmas.

> *First Kiss Podcast wants your first kiss stories! If we choose yours for our special holiday episode, we'll advertise for your business all month long!*

He reached out and plucked the flyer from its tack. He sure as hell didn't have a first kiss story he cared to share, but his grandparents did, and they could use all the help they could get. If he didn't figure out how to get Sleigh Bell Farm making a profit again... Well, he wasn't going to go there. At least not yet. What he wanted now was a beer. And some conversation that didn't include barn repairs.

RACHEL O'ROURKE LOOKED up when the guy in the sheepskin jacket walked in. It was kind of hard not to.

She'd seen him outside the bar doors while she'd been bussing table four. He'd been reading her flyer. And then he'd taken it down and put it in his pocket. Her heart had skipped a beat at that—a handsome young guy responding to her first kiss contest. But then she remembered he was probably taking the flyer because he had a first kiss story to tell. Which meant he was taken. Which meant she needed to concentrate on getting through her shift instead of day-dreaming about first kiss stories, or her podcast finally taking off, or hunky men in Wranglers who looked exactly like young Clint Eastwood with the blue eyes to match.

Picking up a couple of beer mugs with a clink, she re-minded herself she was done with men for a while anyway. She was done with their empty promises and fake declarations of love. And she was *definitely* through with thinking romance was in the cards for her. At least not the kind of romance she talked about on her show. The kind that you bored your grandkids with fifty years later.

Nope. That kind of love she'd just long for from afar. From a safe distance, through her headset and microphone. And maybe a few Hallmark movies on the side. Because, if living vicariously through other people's happily ever afters wasn't what *First Kiss* was all about, well then...

Someone turned on the jukebox, and Bing Crosby's smooth-as-scotch voice unfurled into the bar like a red ribbon. *I'll be home for Christmas...* Rachel wiped down the table and smiled. She loved this song, even though it was bittersweet. It reminded her of her dad. He'd been deployed nearly her entire childhood, and she remembered dancing to it with her mom in their cramped little kitchen. They'd always cried when it came on. She remembered that part vividly.

"Hey, Fancy Face. Look what just walked through those doors."

Rachel turned at the sound of Chloe's voice. Her best friend stood there wearing a Graff t-shirt, size tiny, which stretched over her ample breasts. *Merry Christmas from The Graff! Est. 1884,* it said. But all you could really read was *Christmas from The Graff!* because of the ample breasts thing.

"I saw," Rachel whispered back, hoping Sheepskin Jacket Guy couldn't hear. He'd just sat on a barstool, giving Shane, the bartender, a friendly tug on one of her braids.

Chloe's cranberry red lips stretched into a smile. "Well, maybe there's hope for you yet. You noticed a hot guy. I'm so proud."

"I notice lots of guys."

"No. Them noticing you, and you pretending they don't exist, doesn't count."

"Hmm." Rachel wiped the table down. A soft snow fell outside the windows, making the bar feel cozier than ever. She adored this place, hot guys or no. But what she really wanted to be doing was checking her email for contest submissions.

"Looks like he and Shane are buddies," Chloe said.

"That could work to your advantage."

Rachel didn't look up. Just kept rubbing circles into the already pristine tabletop. "Not interested. But you should go say hi."

"Rachel. Babe." Chloe put her hands on her hips. "I'm not looking for me. I'm looking for you. Trying to save you from becoming Marietta's saddest cat lady, remember?"

"Hey. I love my cat."

"We *all* love our cats, Rach, but they're not supposed to take the place of dating. Or social interaction."

Rachel smiled.

"I know you've sworn off men for a while, but that doesn't mean you can't appreciate from a distance."

"I wouldn't call ten feet a distance."

"I mean, *look* at that guy."

Rachel couldn't help it. She looked up, and to her horror, Sheepskin Jacket Guy was looking back. But, instead of glancing away like most people did when they got caught staring, he grinned at her. And not just any grin either. The slowest, most tantalizing, panty-dropping grin she thought she'd ever seen in her life. There were dimples. And straight white teeth against tanned skin. And stubble. Stubble that she immediately pictured scraping against her most sensitive places. *Dear Lord.*

Cheeks burning, she looked back down at the table.

Chloe laughed. "Definitely hope for you yet."

Chapter Two

RACHEL CURLED UP on the couch and pulled her favorite blanket around her waist. Her cat, whose name was Lucille Ball, and who had the goofball personality to match, jumped up beside her with an expectant meow.

She rubbed Lucy's soft ears and opened her laptop. The light from her little Christmas tree filled the apartment as a gentle snow fell outside. She always put her tree up right after Thanksgiving. By the time Christmas rolled around, it was usually crispy and hanging on by a very thin thread, but she didn't care. Rachel was a total romantic when it came to the holidays. She was that person who drove everyone batty with Christmas music in November—the person who owned more ugly Christmas sweaters than were actually necessary for parties.

Taking a sip of peppermint tea, she opened her email, and smiled when she saw the goldmine of submissions in her inbox. She'd been excited about putting on the contest in honor of Marietta's Support Your Local Business Month. It was a great way to give back to the community she loved so much. But it was also a perfect way to bring new listeners to her podcast. If she played her cards right, and the show took off like she was hoping it would, she might be able to give up waiting tables in a few years and podcast full time. It was a big dream, and one not many people in her life took seriously. Including her own mother. Regardless, it was something she wanted with her whole heart.

Curling into her side, Lucy began a hoarse purr. Rachel reached for her glasses, stuck them on her face, and began reading her emails slowly, carefully. But it wasn't until she got to the one with *My Grandparents' First Kiss* in the subject line that her chest tightened in a hopeful way.

She clicked on it and scrolled down, reading with her breath catching in her throat. By the time she got to the last paragraph, her eyes had filled with tears. *This.* This was what she'd been looking for. A story of true love that had blossomed on the eve of a young man going to war, and of a girl who'd vowed to wait for him back home. In a small ranching community, where they'd eventually come together again to start a life, a business, a family. Their love had lasted all these years. Through children, grandchildren, ups and downs, sickness and health. This was the perfect couple for her Christmas episode. She just knew it.

Rachel hit the reply button and began typing through blurry eyes. *Dear, Lucky...* She didn't stop to let herself wonder about the name, or the images it conjured up—of four-leaf clovers and gold coins. Of someone who'd won the lottery or who never hit two red lights in a row. She just typed the email with only excitement in her heart. *Congratulations on being selected for our first kiss story! When can we meet for our first interview?*

"I'M SORRY, SON. I know this wasn't what you had in mind this Christmas."

Lucky led the little donkey along, looking over at his grandfather and noticing that his limp had gotten more pronounced since the last time he'd been home. Don Elliott had always had a bad knee—an old injury left over from the war, made worse by a lifetime of farm work. He was tough—tougher than most men Lucky knew, but he was also eighty-three, and even though he had regular help with the chores around Sleigh Bell, he was slowing down. Plenty.

"Don't, Gramps," he said. "Don't even think about it, okay?"

His grandpa huffed. He was nearly bald, with two stubborn tufts of hair right above his ears. They were snow white and had shrunk over the years, reminding Lucky of cotton balls. But his blue eyes were sharp as ever in the bright afternoon sunlight, and his mouth curved into a knowing frown.

"It's all your grandmother and I think about. You having to leave school breaks our hearts."

At that, Lucky stopped, the small gray donkey pulling up beside him. Betsy. Betsy the donkey. Her long ears rotated back and forth, zeroing in on the conversation like two fuzzy radars. He stroked her neck with his free hand and looked across the farm to Copper Mountain in the distance. He loved this place. The frosted, rolling hillsides beyond the pastures were like gentle sentences making up a poem. The red barn and the historic Victorian house that he'd spent every childhood summer in, only accentuated the farm's Norman Rockwell charm.

The Elliott land was known far and wide for being some of the prettiest in Montana, and Lucky had always been proud of that. Prouder still of the farm itself and his family's tendency to take in horses and donkeys that had no other place to go. Elderly, lame, or just plain unwanted. Betsy was one of several over the years. The sleigh ride business made them a living, but the animals had always been the heart and soul of Sleigh Bell for Lucky. They were why he was in vet school in the first place. Well, that and the fact that his father expected him to follow in his veterinarian footsteps and solidify his future once and for all.

He looked over at his grandpa in his trademark overalls and muck boots, and his chest felt heavy. His dad couldn't leave his practice in Bozeman to come back to help at Sleigh Bell. And Lucky's brothers had their hands full with their own lives. So, here he was. The youngest of the family. And the least likely to end up being the farm's savior. Because, despite his childhood nickname that said otherwise, he really was *un*lucky at just about everything he touched. But if he was good at anything, it was exuding confidence where there was none.

"Don't worry, Grandpa," he said. "It's only temporary. I've got a plan."

His grandpa chuckled, then coughed. Then pulled his handkerchief out and wiped his mouth. "What's that? Winning the lottery?" He looked over at the barn, and Lucky didn't have to be a mind reader to know he was wondering how the hell they were going to find the money to fix the roof. And the stalls. And the irrigation system.

His grandparents were slowing down. The farm was a lot to keep up with. And even though the family pitched in financially where they could, Sleigh Bell was getting beyond that now. Everyone thought Don and Loretta should probably retire, but nobody had the guts to say it to their faces. And if they did retire, there was nobody waiting in the wings to take over the business. The business they'd worked their entire lives to build, but that was starting to languish needing a facelift of some kind for this new generation of tourists.

"No," Lucky said. "Not the lottery. But don't think I haven't thought about buying a ticket."

"What, then."

"A contest."

His grandpa stared at him. "A contest."

Lucky nodded.

"What kind of contest?"

"A podcast contest. More specifically, a first kiss story *for* a podcast. That's the contest."

"Son, what in God's good name are you talking about?"

Lucky rubbed the back of his neck. It was entirely possible his grandpa would refuse this idea all together. He was a private man. A man of few words. He might not want to tell his story on-air for the entire town to hear. But right now this was their best shot at jumpstarting the business going into the holiday season. Then after that...they'd just have to cross that bridge when they came to it.

"A local podcaster…" He paused and narrowed his eyes at his grandfather. "Do you know what a podcast is?"

"Of course I know what a podcast is. I listen on the iTunes all the time."

Lucky cleared his throat to keep from laughing. "Okay. Well, there's this podcast called First Kiss. Every episode is about a first kiss that led to love or a relationship or something. This podcaster is holding a contest for Support Your Local Business Month, and it's going to be the story for her Christmas episode. The winning submission gets free advertising all December long."

His grandpa whistled under his breath.

"I know. It'd come in handy."

"Did you submit your story then? You got yourself a girl?"

"What?" For some damn reason, his grandparents were obsessed with marrying him off. They'd probably have better luck with that lottery ticket. "No, no, Grandpa. I submitted your story. Yours and Grandma's."

A chilly breeze blew through the pines overhead, and Betsy stomped her foot impatiently, tinkling the bell on her halter.

"Mine and Grandma's…" His grandfather repeated this, letting it sink in. "It *is* a good story…"

"Bet your ass."

"So, what are you saying? Did we win?"

Lucky grinned. So maybe his grandpa wasn't going to be such a hard sell after all. There was a definite twinkle in his eyes.

"Yeah, we did."

"I'll be…"

"So. Free advertising for Sleigh Bell in December. But you have to be on the podcast. And Grandma too. Tell your story. That okay?"

His grandfather patted Betsy. "I think that'll be fine. Just fine. It'll help heading into the tourist season. But after that…"

"We'll figure it out. It'll be okay. It always is."

That wasn't the truth, of course. But it was the kind of thing Lucky said. His way of lightening the load when it got to be too heavy to bear. They both knew their family was on the verge of having to make some decisions about the farm. Decisions that weren't going to be easy. Because it wasn't just the business on the line, or the land. It was the animals too.

"You know, we always hoped you'd want to take over this place someday," his grandfather said. His voice was low. Resigned. Because they'd had this conversation before. Lucky's dad wanted him to be a vet, a professional. His grandparents wanted him to follow his heart. He didn't like to think about it.

He glanced over at the yellow two-story house with the elaborate porch and gingerbread trim. He remembered bottle feeding kittens on that porch. Nursing a sick goat in the yard. So many memories. So many lessons. And his grandpa had been there for every one of them.

"I know," he said. "But it's not that easy. With Dad…"

"He expects too much of you. And you expect too much of yourself. I've never seen anyone with a gift like yours. Never."

Lucky looked away. He didn't like these talks. Because they always made him feel like he was giving up on something, but he didn't know what.

"If I have any kind of gift, I can put it to good use being a vet."

"That's true. But we just thought…"

Betsy shook her head and tugged on the lead rope. She was ready for lunch, and Lucky couldn't blame her. His own stomach had started growling half an hour ago.

His grandpa sighed. "Never mind what we thought. You'll be a good vet, son. A real good vet."

They began walking toward the barn again. Toward the stalls with the broken slats and the roof that leaked in the rain. Being a vet would provide a solid future, Lucky thought. As great as Sleigh Bell was, as much as he coveted this place, its future was anything but solid.

Chapter Three

R ACHEL TURNED HER Honda onto the bumpy country drive that led to the beautiful house in the distance. She passed a carved wood sign that read, *Welcome to Sleigh Bell Farm, Where it's Christmas All Year Long!*

She smiled, barely able to contain her excitement. This was it—the morning of her first interview with the Elliott family. She'd carefully prepared her questions the night before and had switched shifts with Chloe to have the day off, in case the interview ran long.

Glancing over at the passenger's seat where her brand new microphone sat, she touched it affectionately. Then looked out the window as the car bounced over a few ruts in the road. The view was breathtaking. Since picking Don and Loretta Elliott's story for her contest, she'd done some research on their family farm. The land had been claimed at the turn of the century and the iconic house built not long after. But the sleigh ride business that had put the farm itself on the map had been launched after Don and Loretta married in 1954.

There had been ups and downs over the years—they'd had four sons, one of whom had been killed in a car accident in the 1980s. The other three boys had various ties to the business, but as far as she could tell, none of them were physically involved with the farm anymore. Except for their grandson, who'd sent their story in, and who she was getting ready to meet in person, it sounded like they were on their own running the place. Something she had to assume might be coming to an end soon with them being in their early eighties.

She drove under a row of big maple trees, their branches naked for winter. Big rolling pastures stretched on either side of the car, surrounded by white fences that were in need of paint, but were more charming because of it.

To her right, a chestnut horse raised its head from grazing as she passed, eyeing the car with lazy interest. Puffy white clouds moved over a sky so blue it hurt her eyes.

Rachel pulled slowly up to the house and put the car in park. A small tan dog ran out, barking and wagging its stubby tail.

"Stitch! Come!"

She cut the engine and looked up at the sound of the booming male voice, expecting...she didn't know what exactly. Since getting Lucky Elliott's first kiss submission last week, she'd been having trouble picturing him. His emails had been warm, funny. Well written. He'd mentioned being home from graduate school, so she wasn't surprised at how intelligent he sounded. She guessed she'd pictured a nerdy farmer type. A cowlick, maybe glasses. Cute, but not too cute.

The man coming down the porch steps was *not* a nerdy

farmer. Tall, broad shouldered. Loose-fitting jeans and old cowboy boots…a sheepskin jacket with the collar high around his neck.

Her heart fluttered in her chest as she reached for the door. *Sheepskin Jacket Guy.* Of course. He'd grabbed a flyer that day. She'd been too thrown by the nickname to tie him to her contest winner. She realized now that he was even more gorgeous up close and doing funny things to her ovaries as she managed to step out of the car without turning an ankle.

The scruffy little dog wiggled at her feet, and she laughed, bending down to pet it.

"Careful. He'll lick you to death." Sheepskin Jacket Guy smiled, and she nearly forgot to breathe. She also forgot that she wasn't supposed to be interested in men at the moment. But her stupid heart was there to remind her with every clunky beat.

Looking up, she saw his eyes were an even deeper blue than she remembered from the Graff that day. But his hair was the same, catching the light of the morning sun like copper. It was all making it hard to find the right words to introduce herself. Thankfully, he seemed to sense her nerves, which was mortifying and a godsend all at once, and he introduced himself first.

Reaching out a big hand, he stepped forward. She caught the faint scent of soap and man on the chilly December breeze, and goosebumps rose on her arms.

"Rachel?"

She smiled back and nodded, putting her hand in his,

and letting herself revel in the feel of his skin against hers. It was rough, calloused. The skin of a man who worked outside for a living.

"I'm Lucky. Lucky Elliot," he said. "Nice to meet you."

"Nice to meet you, too." She let go and hugged herself awkwardly. "It's just beautiful out here."

"It's prettier with fresh snow. And in the spring when everything is green. But we'll take it."

He said this all while keeping his steady, warm gaze on her. She got the feeling he didn't get nervous often. In fact, he was probably in his element—flustering a woman with his sex appeal and watching her catch fire underneath that gaze.

Running her hand over her knit scarf, she reminded herself she was a professional. Here as a podcaster with a story to record. He was the winner of her contest, or his grandparents were, and that was it. Still, she found herself instantly curious about him. What he was going to school for, how long he'd be back in Marietta, what kind of connection he really had to this farm, and did he have a future here?

"My grandparents are excited to meet you," he said, bending down to grab a stick that the dog had deposited at his feet. He straightened again and threw it a country mile. Not surprising, since he had the body of a long, lean baseball player.

She grinned, watching the dog go bounding toward the barn, the stick finally landing in a pile of hay outside its big double doors. "Does he always bring it back?"

"Always. He's got a one-track mind. Unless he gets distracted by the chickens. Or the chicken poop, I should say.

He has an unfortunate habit of rolling in it. It's his kryptonite."

Laughing, she looked up at him and shielded her eyes from the sun. "I guess there are worse things."

"I've never met a woman okay with rolling in chicken poop. Stitch has found his people."

"Do what makes you happy. That's my motto."

He watched her for another few seconds, his wide mouth tilting slightly. She had no idea what he was thinking, but she had the feeling she'd said something right.

"So," she said, clearing her throat. "I brought my equipment..." Her ears burned. That was stretching it. Her microphone that she'd bought on Amazon wasn't really heavy-duty podcast material, but she was excited about using it. And getting to say things like *equipment*. And following people around with it in tow.

"Great. Is the kitchen okay?"

"Of course. And your grandparents are inside?"

"They are. And there might be some cookies waiting for you. Sorry about that. I know the sun's barely up, but it's how my grandma rolls."

Rachel's heart squeezed. Her grandparents had died when she was little. She'd spent her childhood longing for things like milk and cookies set out on chipped platters.

She tucked her long bangs behind her ear as the breeze kicked up again. "Cookies for breakfast actually sounds like the best thing ever."

"It really does, doesn't it?"

They smiled at each other as Stitch began barking at a

vehicle coming up the drive.

Rachel turned to see a big, blue truck pulling a horse trailer behind it. "Are you expecting company?"

Lucky frowned. For the first time, she noticed the pink, slightly puckered skin at the base of his throat. What looked like scar tissue. "No," he said. "I'm not. But this might take a few minutes. Are you in a hurry?"

Leaving was the farthest thing from her mind. She was glad she'd taken the day off, so they didn't have to rush it. "Not at all. Don't worry about me, I know it's a working day for you."

Before he could reply, the truck door opened, and an older woman hopped out. She was platinum blonde, a shade of tan usually reserved for July, and wore a huge rhinestone belt buckle that sparkled in the sun.

She grinned and walked over with Stitch dancing around her boots. "Lucky Elliott, you handsome devil. Don said you were coming back to help for a while. You're an angel, hon." She looked over at Rachel then, and smiled slowly. "And who's this pretty thing? You finally let someone catch you for once?"

Rachel's cheeks burned. "Oh! Uh…no. I'm just…"

"Damn, Lou," Lucky said. "She just got here. And no, we're not together."

Rachel didn't think her heart could've beat any faster, but it went ahead and picked up a notch anyway. No, they definitely weren't together. But the thought of it happily lodged itself in her brain. To torment her later, no doubt.

Lou shook her head. "Shame."

"Rachel O'Rourke," he said, "meet Lou Bianchi, a family friend."

Lou reached over and gave Rachel's hand a hearty shake. She liked the older woman immediately. It was impossible not to.

"Nice to meet you, honey," Lou said. "And don't let him fool you. He *can* be caught. Just hasn't met anyone with a strong enough lasso yet."

"What can I do for you, Lou?" Lucky asked. "Since I'm guessing you didn't come all the way out here for the charming banter."

As if on cue, whatever was in the trailer kicked at the wall, earning a bark from Stitch.

"Stitch," Lucky said. "Go lie down."

The little dog plopped down in the mud puddle where he'd been standing and scratched behind his ear.

Lou planted her hands on her narrow hips. "Well, I was hoping you'd be able to help me out with this one, hon. I'm in a pickle here."

Lucky stepped up to the trailer and looked through the slats. Rachel could only see the tops of two black ears and some tangled forelock. There was another hard knock on the inside of the trailer and a shrill whinny.

"Oh, shit," Lucky breathed.

"Yeah. He's in bad shape."

"Where'd you get him?"

"He's an owner surrender. The county was gonna take him, but with some persuasion on my part, the family gave him up to me first. I drive by their place every day on my way home, and it just broke my heart. They couldn't take care of him, that's obvious. Took me nearly twenty minutes to get him loaded up. He's scared to death. Who knows how long it's been since he's been loved on. Maybe never."

Rachel could see Lucky's jaw muscles clench underneath the rough, reddish brown stubble. He shoved a hand through his hair, his jacket riding up to expose a sliver of muscled abdomen and what looked like more scar tissue. She forced her gaze away.

"I'm getting ready to take a cruise for Christmas," Lou said. "I won't be around for two weeks, or I'd bring him out to my place. I was hoping…"

Lucky nodded. "Of course we'll take him."

"I know you have a lot on your plate, kiddo. But I just couldn't leave him there."

"No. I know. We'll look him over, make sure he doesn't have anything else going on, other than the malnutrition and neglect. Hopefully, we can get some weight on him and start working on the trust issues. Maybe we'll get him rehomed by spring."

"And I can help with that. I know plenty of folks who'd be in the market for a nice little horse like this. He's got a brand. Looks like a mustang."

Rachel watched, taking it all in. Getting a feel for what this farm was all about. There were the sleigh rides in the winter on the snowy streets of Marietta. The carriage rides in the summer underneath the evergreens.

She knew that part just by living here. But the other stuff—she'd had to dig a little deeper for that. Common sense told her the Elliott's were burning the candle at both ends. If Lucky's grandparents were getting close to retirement, and they were using their time and resources caring for even a few homeless animals, there probably wasn't a ton left over for the business. Her heart wrenched at that. It was an all-too-common American story. Family farms like this struggled if the economy was shaky, or if the kids and grandkids wanted to follow a different path in life. Farms like Sleigh Bell ended up going on life support and then, slowly, painfully, dying off.

Lucky walked around to the back of the trailer and opened its heavy doors. Rachel held her breath as the horse kicked at the trailer wall. But Lucky stepped up and disappeared inside—tall, broad shouldered, confident.

Lou looked over, a couple of tiny Christmas trees dangling from her earlobes that Rachel hadn't noticed before.

"Have you ever seen Lucky work with animals, hon?" Lou asked, her voice deep and throaty.

"I haven't. We just met today, actually."

"Huh," Lou said, smiling. "I could've sworn by the way he was looking at you…"

How had he been looking at her? Rachel thought she'd been the only one doing the looking.

"Well, then," Lou said. "You're in for a treat. He has a way with horses. Some people think that's how he got his nickname—he's had a couple of close calls. A stallion almost bit clean through his arm last year. But I like to think it has more to do with the ladies, if you ask me." She crossed her arms over her chest, eyeing Rachel. "And you two *just* met today?"

The horse whinnied again, pawing at the trailer floor. They could hear Lucky's soothing voice coming from inside, too low to make out the words.

Willing her heartbeat to slow, she smiled at Lou. "You know, I haven't gotten around to asking him...what's his real name?" All of a sudden, the need to know was so overpowering, it made her chest tight. They *had* only just met, but it was becoming more and more obvious this man had a story to tell. Stories usually revealed themselves by peeling away layer after layer. She could see Lucky Elliott's layers, and then some.

Lou opened her mouth to answer, but before she could, the horse whinnied again. He tossed his head, but this time took a step back. And then another, his hooves clunking hollowly on the trailer floor.

Lucky continued talking in low tones and, after a few seconds, Rachel could see painfully thin hindquarters emerge in the morning sunlight. A dull, black coat stretched over bone. There were open sores on the animal's coat and mud caked all over his quivering legs.

She gasped.

"I'll never understand people," Lou muttered. "Never, as long as I live."

Lucky backed the horse down the ramp the rest of the way. "That's it," he said, running a hand over the matted mane. "Nobody's gonna hurt you. You're safe here."

The horse's eyes were wide, almost rolling. But, when Lucky spoke, he visibly steadied, letting himself be comforted. Like he'd been waiting for this kindness for a very long time.

As Rachel watched, something funny happened to her heart. She was aware of it growing, stretching, as she stood there. Over the last few months, and after the last breakup with a man who cared more about his truck than her, she'd convinced herself the only decent guys out there were the subjects of her podcast. Husbands, boyfriends, lovers, who belonged to other women. It was a defense mechanism, she knew that. It's what got her through. Because, deep down, she was the worst kind of romantic. She believed in love. And despite what she tried to tell herself, she believed there *were* good guys out there.

Lucky was a good guy. In the flesh. And watching him move his hands over the horse's back, she opened herself to the idea of him. Of his story. Of his grandparents' story. And found that she couldn't wait to tell it.

"He'll be a wonderful vet," Lou said softly.

"Oh," Rachel breathed. "I didn't know that's what he wanted to do. It makes sense now. He's so good at this."

Stitch trotted over and dropped the stick hopefully at Lou's feet. She bent to scratch behind his ears, and he closed his eyes in pure doggie rapture.

"But he won't be able to work the farm too," Lou said. "Damn shame. I'm afraid it'll be the end of this place."

Chapter Four

THEY ALL SAT around the antique dining room table, the rooster-shaped clock above the stove ticking off the seconds in the background. Lucky's grandmother was in the middle of the story about how she and his grandpa met. There were warm peanut butter cookies on the table, along with chilled milk in snowman mugs. But all Lucky could concentrate on was the woman sitting across from him.

She was beautiful. But not in an uppity kind of way. Beautiful in a girl next door kind of way, with a small, slightly upturned nose, and freckles scattered haphazardly across her cheeks. Her silky brown hair fell just past her collar bone, and she wore it straight, plain. As if she didn't want to bring any attention to herself. But it wasn't working. He was having a hard time not staring at her as his grandma spoke.

Still, she'd caught him looking a few times, and she smiled, obviously embarrassed. Of course she would be. He was acting like a teenage boy. But he really couldn't help it— he liked the color her skin turned when she blushed. The way she lowered her lashes and looked at her hands folded in front of her. The way she'd bring her plump bottom lip between her teeth for just a second, as if gathering herself.

"She told me she didn't go out with boys she didn't know," his grandpa was saying, chuckling and leaning back in his chair. "And I said, how was she supposed to get to know me if she wouldn't go out with me?"

Rachel glanced back and forth between them, smiling. She'd told him in that first email that these stories gave her faith in humanity. She'd admitted to being a little jaded in other areas of her life, but that she loved hearing about romance in all its forms. Sitting here now, watching her brown eyes warm at his grandpa's words, he could tell she'd chosen to tell him something intimate about herself. And he liked that, too.

He took a bite of warm cookie, then washed it down with a swallow of milk.

"And your anniversary is in August?" Rachel asked, repositioning her microphone in front of his grandmother.

"August ninth. It'll be sixty-five years. A lot of ups and downs, but I wouldn't change a thing."

His grandpa reached across the table and put his wrinkled hand over hers. "And neither would I, honey."

Rachel smiled and wrote something down on her notepad. "And this farm," she said, looking back up. "This is obviously your life's work. Tell me a little about that."

Lucky's grandma caught his eye for a second. There seemed to be so many unspoken things between them these days. A heaviness that hadn't been there before he started graduate school. The farm was the elephant in the room. Its survival, or its death, settling squarely on all their shoulders.

Running a hand over her short, gray hair, his grandmother settled her gaze on Rachel again. She looked much like the quintessential sweet old lady in her homemade apron with the pears all over it. But Lucky knew better. She was just as tough as her husband. Tougher in a lot of ways. Out here, you had to be. But there was no mistaking the sadness in her expression right then, and Lucky felt its heaviness all the way to his bones.

"This farm," she said, her voice suddenly hoarse. "It's our baby."

Rachel nodded, and Lucky watched her closely for understanding. It was more than their baby. The farm was the heartbeat of their family.

"I can see how much you love it," Rachel said.

"Seventy-two acres," his grandpa said. "Been in our family for generations. The business, though. We struggle sometimes. It doesn't pay the bills like it used to. There are a lot of competitors around Marietta where there didn't used to be. Have you seen that bicycle contraption that holds a dozen people? The tourists peddle it all over town, visiting local bars—the Graff and Greys. A lot cheaper to own and operate than a sleigh and a team of donkeys."

"Oh, I've seen that thing," Rachel said. "But I'm old fashioned. I love the idea of a sleigh ride through town."

"We do it up right, sweetie," Lucky's grandma said, putting another cookie on Rachel's plate. "Hot cocoa, and blankets in case you get cold. And Dave and Betsy have the cutest harnesses. We had them made years ago. Just as cute as a button."

"Dave and Betsy?"

"They're our donkey team," Lucky said. "They're old, so they'll be retiring soon, and our horses will take over. But Dave and Betsy are the stars of the show. Without them, the sleigh and carriage rides won't be the same."

Rachel licked her lips and wrote something down on her notepad.

Sitting back in his chair, Lucky continued watching her. There were so many things about Sleigh Bell that were changing right before their eyes. Saying them out loud, telling them to a woman who was a stranger, but felt like something else, was like admitting something he'd been denying for a long time. Life as they knew it, as they'd loved it, was going to be shifting soon. Lucky had never been overly emotional, approaching his days with the matter-of-fact disposition he got from his dad. But this…this made his throat ache in a way that made him swallow and look away.

His grandmother was feeling it too. She'd put her hands in her lap and was smoothing her apron. Her eyes were undeniably misty.

At the sudden silence that had settled over the room, Rachel looked up from her notepad. Then flipped a switch on her microphone and put it down on the table. "I think that's probably enough for today. You've all been so wonderful letting me come out and take up a whole morning."

"Is that all you need, honey?" his grandma said, sounding a little disappointed. Lucky had a feeling she liked this. All of it. Having a young woman sitting at her kitchen table. Talking about the good old days. Getting to serve milk in her favorite Christmas mugs. She didn't get the company out here that she probably craved.

"Well, if you don't mind, I'd love to come out again. This is a special episode, so it's going to be a two-parter. The more I talk to you all, the better."

"How do you have time for this?" his grandmother asked. "If you don't mind me asking. Don't you have a day job too?"

"I do. I'm a server at the Graff, but I'm hoping to be able to podcast full time in a couple of years. I've gotten fortunate with a few local sponsors. Sweet Pea Flowers and Copper Mountain Chocolate Shop. Everyone has been really supportive. I think people like the idea of falling in love. Even the super tough cowboys around here." She smiled then. "But I'm not sure how many of them listen to my podcast."

Lucky let that settle. This wasn't a dream most people would have the courage to wrap both arms around. But here she was. With that microphone she was so obviously proud of and eyes that sparkled with excitement. Something inside him warmed at that. And then, just as suddenly, he pushed the feeling away. Dreams were risky. They were good ways to get yourself in trouble—emotionally and otherwise. He'd never let himself dream fully, because his parents hadn't wanted a dreamer for their youngest son. And Lucky could understand that. Really, he could.

"Well," his grandma said, "we're sure glad you chose us for your special Christmas episode. The advertising will be such a help."

Rachel sat up straight, her small diamond earrings sparkling under the light. "You know, it's just a thought, but have you ever entered a tree in Mistletoe and Montana? The Christmas tree auction?"

Lucky cleared his throat. "Actually, I've been trying to get them to enter for years. It's for a great cause..."

Rachel nodded, excitedly. "It really is. It's being held here again, so all the proceeds go to Marietta General."

"And the exposure for local businesses is huge this time of year," Lucky said. "People come from all over Montana. People with deep pockets, looking for things to do while they're in town. That, combined with the boost of social media, could really help promote the farm. A few solid weeks of booked trips would carry us into January. Maybe even February and Valentine's Day weekend."

His grandpa sighed, furrowing his thick brows. "We need a good Christmas season to be able to get you back to school for the spring semester."

Lucky would never say it, but he also needed to get back to work. He made a vow a long time ago not to rely on his father for school. His grandfather was paying him, but he felt guilty about that when the farm hands had to be paid, too. Lucky's job at the feed store in Bozeman was perfect and would help get him through the next few years at the university with minimal help from his family. He was only twenty-five, but sometimes felt more like sixty-five with trying to juggle all this.

Rachel looked over at him, and there was something in her expression that made him feel like she knew exactly what he'd been thinking just now.

"You should enter," she said softly. "I think Sleigh Bell should definitely have a tree there. Your family has had such an impact on this town for so many years, it's only right that you have an entry."

He shifted his gaze to his grandparents. "What do you think?"

"Mistletoe and Montana falls about a week before Christmas this year," Rachel said. "That means you could even incorporate it into the podcast if you wanted. Might be a nice way to wrap up the episode."

Lucky's grandma tapped her lips with her index finger, something she did when she was considering something. "I think it's a good idea, kids. I really do."

"Great!" Rachel smiled over at him. And he didn't like the immediate physical reaction he felt. Dry throat, tight chest. Heartbeat tapping in his neck.

Lucky was in the middle of trying to prove something to everyone in his life right now. That he was his own man. That he was serious about his future. And another fling with a girl he barely knew couldn't be part of that equation. He was tired of crashing right out of the gate. He wanted more.

And despite the look Rachel O'Rourke was giving him right now, she deserved more too.

Chapter Five

"GIRL, GET *OVER* here!"

Rachel laughed. It was hard not to. Her friend Bob, who worked the front desk at the Graff, had an infectious personality. The loud Christmas sweaters, the light-up ties, the holiday pins for his lapel that he must've raided every church bazaar for this side of this Mississippi. It was all part of his charm. Bob *loved* Christmas.

She headed over to where he stood beside a plate of sugar cookies that he'd probably baked himself. There was a fresh garland hanging from the front desk with tiny white lights woven throughout. Holiday elevator music played softly in the background, and the smell of newly brewed coffee teased her early morning, caffeine-deprived senses.

"I'm not sure everyone heard you, Bob."

He cocked his head and looked her up and down. "Something's different about you."

She glanced down at her outfit, which consisted of boots, jeans, a red wool jacket, and a white scarf. And a beanie that she'd knitted last Saturday night with Lucille Ball on her lap, instead of going out with Chloe to Greys, where all the ranchers hung out on the weekends. It was Chloe's happy place, and she never got tired of trying to drag Rachel along. Which was a losing battle.

"What? I look the same as always."

"Nope. No." He nodded politely to a man in a crisp suit walking past. "Good morning, sir." Then turned his attention back to her. "Spill."

"Bob," she said, trying not to smile, which would only encourage him. "I have to get to work."

"Shane won't give a rip if you're a few minutes late."

"I beg to differ."

"You can differ all you want. Doesn't hide that look on your face."

"What look?"

"The happy one. The one that says *man*."

"What?" She brushed some imaginary lint off her coat. "I don't know what you're talking about."

"Oh my god, Rach. You're the worst liar."

"I'm not lying."

Bob rolled his eyes.

"I'm not!"

"I heard about your new podcast episode. Featuring the Elliotts. Featuring *Lucky* Elliott."

"It's not featuring Lucky Elliot. It's featuring his grandparents. His sweet, elderly grandparents and their first kiss story. And how do you know Lucky Elliott?"

Bob laughed like a mischievous elf. An elf with male pattern baldness and a paunch. The only thing missing were the pointed ears. "Oh, come *on*. I can't believe *you* don't know who he is."

"No…I mean, I might've heard some things."

"Okay, let's see what you might've heard." He held up an index finger. "One. A total heartbreaker. I mean…"

She watched him, determined not to agree. Which she absolutely wanted to.

He held up another finger. "Two. The star quarterback at Marietta High. They still talk about that arm in practices."

"I didn't go to high school here, so…"

"Three. The most eligible bachelor in three counties. Three. *Counties.*"

This time she couldn't help it—she grinned. "Maybe he is, *Robert.* But for other kinds of girls. Girls like Chloe, or…I don't know. But he's a heartbreaker, you said it yourself. And if there's one thing I don't need, it's another guy like that."

"Ahh. So you've thought about it."

"You're impossible. I'm going to work."

Turning on her heel, she heard him call after her. "Chloe told me he invited you to Mistletoe and Montana! That requires a dress, you know. I'll help you shop!"

She waved over her shoulder. Chloe couldn't be trusted, it was official. But her balding front desk cupid was right—going to the auction would require a dress. Which felt enough like a date to make her toes curl inside her sensible canvas Keds.

When it came right down to it though, it didn't matter. Because what she'd told Bob was true. She wasn't in the market for falling for a complicated man. And even though she wouldn't necessarily categorize Lucky as complicated, she *would* categorize him as more complicated than she was used to. And maybe that had everything to do with the fact that she hadn't been able to stop thinking about him since yesterday. Since seeing him put his hands on that poor horse or smile at her over his grandparents scarred oak table. Maybe her own feelings were the complication.

She walked into the century-old bar, and waved at Shane, who was signing for a beer delivery. A big Christmas tree glowed in the corner, trimmed in its traditional amber lights and shot glasses. She really did love this place. She loved its history, its elegant beauty. Loved serving the locals and tourists, talking to them and hearing their stories. But she was so ready for something else. That dream that she'd been reaching for ever since she'd heard her first podcast. She was ready for her own story to unfold.

It was funny. When she'd been telling Lucky about her podcast yesterday, she'd seen something on his face that looked familiar somehow. At the time, she just thought he'd understood how she felt. But now, she wondered if he understood on a deeper level. Was being a vet his highest aspiration? He must be passionate about that, but how passionate? And how did he feel about the farm that had been in his family for a lifetime? Who, if anyone, was going to take it over one day?

All these questions and more had been swirling in her brain for the last twenty-four hours, and she knew why. It had everything to do with wanting to peel back those layers that made Lucky who he was. It really wasn't just Don and Loretta's first kiss story that was going to make this episode special. It was the story about what had happened after that first kiss—to the kids they'd raised, the grandkids who'd come along, the animals they'd saved. And the farm that they'd so lovingly cared for over the years. Lucky was part of that. A big part of it.

She hung her purse up in the back room and took off her coat. Then stood there for a minute, looking out the old, single-pane windows to Front Avenue where people walked, bundled up against the cold. And beyond that, to the mountains in the distance that looked like they'd been turned upside down and dipped in powdered sugar.

She breathed deeply, smelling the beer-battered onion rings cooking in the kitchen, and her stomach growled. Crossing her arms over her chest, she knew what she *wanted* to do. She wanted to get Lucky to tell her everything. Or everything he was willing to share. She wanted this episode to be one of her most heartfelt, and, in order to do that, she needed to put herself out there a little. And she told herself it had nothing to do with how blue his eyes were or how his shirt stretched just right over his broad shoulders. It only had to do with the story. That was it.

Biting the inside of her cheek, she dug her phone out of her purse. She brought Lucky's name up and texted him before she could talk herself out of it.

I'd really love to get more of your perspective for the podcast. I'll be recording soon. Have time for coffee?

She hit send with butterflies bumping around in her lower belly. Then, before she could put her phone back in her purse, it dinged with a reply.

Riding out tomorrow to check the fences. Want to come? We can bring thermoses for the coffee.

She looked out the window again and smiled slowly. She truly did want more of his perspective for the podcast. But those broad shoulders didn't hurt any.

LUCKY LED NICK, their sweetest and oldest gelding, over to Rachel, trying not to notice how tight her jeans were. How the denim moved over every soft curve.

"He's beautiful," Rachel said, tucking her hair behind her ears. "And tall."

"He is tall, but he's bombproof, I promise. He'll take good care of you." Lucky patted the palomino's neck, and dust puffed into the morning air.

"It's been a long time since I've been on a horse."

"It's like riding a bike," he said. "It'll come back. But you might be sore in the morning."

She smiled over at him, but he could tell she was nervous. And there was no way she was getting her foot in that stirrup without splitting those jeans right down the crotch.

"Come here," he said, keeping one hand on the horse's shoulders.

She stepped toward him, and he caught her scent on the chilly breeze. Something light and faintly floral. It made his stomach tighten. Her dark hair shone under the sun, strands of it moving over her face and prompting her to push it away again.

When she was close enough, he reached behind her and put a hand on her lower back. She startled, then realized he was getting her in a position to help her up.

"Here you go," he said, facing her toward the saddle. Nick shifted, and the leather creaked as Rachel grabbed the horn.

Lucky bent, lacing his hands together. She stepped in the makeshift stirrup, and he lifted her up until she could swing her leg over Nick's back.

When she seemed satisfied the horse wasn't going to bolt, she took a deep breath and settled herself in the saddle. "I should've worn different jeans," she said, looking down at him. "Habit. These are my favorites."

He adjusted her foot in the stirrup, not trusting himself to hold that chocolate gaze any longer than he needed to. "Nicky doesn't mind. And neither do I."

"Admit it," she said. "You were waiting for them to rip, weren't you?"

He did look up then, squinting into the sun. "No, ma'am."

"Liar."

"Okay. Maybe."

She laughed. "They still might, if this ride gets bouncy."

He immediately pictured her bouncing. *All* of her bouncing, and then his own jeans felt too tight.

"If they rip," he said, "or if things get uncomfortable, let me know. I don't want you suffering in silence."

"I know we don't know each other very well, but suffering in silence isn't my specialty."

"Oh, yeah?"

"Yeah. I have a tendency to complain a little. But I promise I'll be on my best behavior."

He didn't want her on her best behavior. He wanted her to feel comfortable with him, although why he cared so much, he had no idea. She was right. They really didn't know each other. At least not well enough for him to be imagining the things he was now, like what it would feel like to haul her off Nick and pull her close. So close those jeans would be the only thing between them.

He clenched his teeth and handed her the reins. "Here you go. Probably won't need them, though. He'll just follow alongside Pop Tart."

Rachel's lips curved. "Pop Tart?"

Lucky walked over to the paint mare that he'd had since he was seventeen and untied her from the hitching post. "She used to have this thing when she was a baby. Where she'd spook if something startled her. Except she'd just pop straight up in the air. It's actually how we ended up with her. Her owners were getting tired of falling off."

"And you don't fall off?"

"I *have* fallen off. But I don't make a habit of it."

"I heard you actually did some amateur rodeo a few years back?"

He hoisted himself in the saddle, the sharp smell of leather and horse as familiar to him as anything. Looking over at Rachel, he winked. "You heard right."

"So, what happened? With the rodeo stuff?"

He nudged Pop Tart toward the pastures, and Nick fell

in step beside her, their frosty breath puffing into the air. The hollow clop of the horses' hooves was a cadence he never tired of. Rachel's leg brushed against his, and he was more than aware of the simple contact. Everything with her seemed magnified. Even the feel of the winter sun on the back of his neck was warmer, sweeter with her next to him. Probably because she had a way of making him see the farm like he was seeing it for the first time. Through her eyes. And he liked how it looked through her eyes.

"I realized even with the nickname, I'd end up breaking my damn neck," he said. "I like the rodeo. My brother Jake's still on the circuit. But I never felt that's what I was best at. I ended up spending most of my time in the paddocks with the horses. It was pretty clear from the beginning I wasn't going to make a great cowboy. At least not in that sense."

"So, vet school?"

He reached down and rubbed Pop Tart's fuzzy neck, straightening his thoughts out before answering. They were getting to know each other, but he also knew she was gathering information. And that anything he said today could be used in the podcast later. She'd been very clear about that, and he'd understood. But this was a subject he wasn't sure he'd come to terms with yet. Not deep down, anyway.

"Yeah. But, growing up, I never really saw myself as vet material. Even though that's what my dad is and we knew he wanted us to follow in his footsteps."

"You and your brothers?"

He nodded. "They're scattered now. But they still feel a

connection with this place—with Marietta in general. I think they'll be back eventually. It's in our blood."

The horses headed down a slight embankment where the grass was taller and big pine trees peppered the property. Lucky scanned the fencing as Lou's little black mustang trotted up and whinnied a greeting. He'd been eating well, and Lucky was relieved to find that, other than the malnutrition, he didn't have any lasting damage. He'd been calling him Dreamer. It seemed to fit.

"He seems so much better!" Rachel said. "Skinny, but better."

"I think he is. Animals can sense when they've been rescued from a bad situation. They're almost grateful."

As he said it, the horse tossed his head and trotted playfully along the fence line. The tangles were gone from his mane, and his dark coat was free of mud. Lucky had spent a few hours on him the other day, and he was already getting attached. A hazard of the job.

Rachel laughed. "He seems happy here."

Lucky nodded, wondering for a second how the little horse would take to a harness and sleigh. And then dismissed the idea just as quickly. He wasn't in any position to be making decisions beyond the next few months. Who knew where they'd be by then?

"I've always wanted a place to call home," Rachel said.

He looked over, but she kept gazing straight ahead. Enjoying the mountain view, or avoiding looking back, he couldn't tell. But there was definitely a tone to her voice that he hadn't heard before.

"I know you didn't grow up here…" he said. They were about the same age. And he would've noticed her in high school, for sure.

She shook her head as her body swayed with Nick's big strides. She had a natural seat. She looked at home on a horse. He wondered if anyone had ever told her that before.

"No," she said. "I was an Army brat. We moved all over the country—Hawaii, California, you name it, before Mom and I finally settled in Marietta for good. She and my dad divorced, and we had an elderly aunt here, so it seemed like as good a place as any. And we loved it right away, so…"

"I'm sorry. About the divorce part."

Shrugging, she did look over then. And her eyes were masking something, he could tell. Like she wanted to talk about it, but she was afraid to. "It is what it is. My dad wasn't faithful, and my mom never trusted him after that. It was better for them to split than keep living a lie. It was hard on me, though. I was so starry-eyed growing up. Read every single romance novel my mom ever owned. Without her knowing, of course." She smiled. "But it planted a seed in me, I guess. The love. The devotion. I never stopped wanting it for her."

"And what about the podcasting?" he asked. "When did that become a thing?"

A couple of ducks flew by overhead, and Rachel glanced up before answering. "Well, I went to community college in Bozeman. I had no idea what I wanted to do, only that I wanted to start spreading my wings a little. And my friend mentioned listening to podcasts on her way to work, so I started listening on the way to school. And from school. And on the weekends and at night when I was cleaning my apartment and on walks. I was hooked."

"I listened to that one you told me about." He snapped his fingers. "Where the guy was wrongfully accused of murder?"

"Yes! That's one of my favorites. The host is so good. The way she interviews her guests, the way she delves into each episode." She paused, shifting in her saddle. "It's an art form, a way of telling a story that people can relate to. A way to reach them and make a difference, even if it's a small one. At least that's how I like to think about it."

He watched her, and there was a funny feeling inside his chest. Because he could tell this was what she loved most, and she was choosing to pursue it. Even though it was risky. Even though most people probably wouldn't think it was a serious ambition. But to hell with them. There was undeniable pride in her voice. And, all of a sudden, he recognized the feeling for what it was—a combination of deep admiration. And envy.

"Can I ask you a question?" she said.

"Shoot."

"Why do they call you Lucky?"

The question, like always, was a punch to the gut. But she had no way of knowing that. To Rachel, it was a natural question, like asking someone's middle name. And he really didn't understand why it affected him like this, all these years later. He had a stock answer—one that satisfied people and kept his memories, his pain, at arm's length.

But, riding alongside Rachel under the bright December sun, he felt like that stock answer was a copout. A way of avoiding who he really was. Because avoidance was the easiest thing. Always had been.

He rubbed his chin, which was rough with stubble. "It's probably not what you think."

He felt the weight of her gaze like a lead ball, even though he knew she didn't mean anything by it. Lucky had stuff to work through, and this was a good reminder. Still, he'd rather kick Pop Tart into a gallop and leave the question and all its intricacies behind.

Instead, he grit his teeth and pulled the horse to a stop. Nick stopped, too, and Rachel frowned, watching him.

"See the barn? Below that ridge?"

She looked over and nodded.

"That's not the original barn. The original burned when I was a kid."

"Oh," she breathed. Then looked back at him, her brows furrowed.

"I was inside at the time."

"What?"

He nodded. "I was ten. Playing with some leftover sparklers, which I knew were off-limits. When you grow up on just under eighty acres, and your older brothers are off doing other things, you get creative with your time. I got creative. And stupid."

She didn't smile. Didn't talk. She seemed to sense the delicacy of what he was about to say and waited.

He swallowed hard, feeling the memory of that day

squeeze him like a cold fist. But it wasn't just the memory of the day itself—the smell of smoke, the panic in his father's eyes, the sound of flames roaring toward the sky. It was the feeling of shame and disappointment that he'd carried with him for the next fourteen years of his life.

"I set the hay loft on fire." He paused, realizing he hadn't spoken the words aloud in a very long time. He'd gotten good at not thinking about it, always wearing a t-shirt in the summers, even when working in the heat. And when a girlfriend would eventually ask about the scars, he'd deflect like always. Then, he'd find a reason to move on. To make a joke about his lack of commitment and walk out the door. Lucky was a living, breathing, self-fulfilling prophecy. If you told yourself you were a screw-up enough, you started believing it.

Rachel sat quietly on Nick as he lowered his head to graze. For some reason, her silence made him want to tell her more. Maybe because, with her, he didn't feel so much like a screw-up, than as a man who was trying to negotiate his future and all the complexity that went with it.

"The barn went up so fast," he said, "that I really don't have too much memory of what happened next. Only bits and pieces. But I do remember my dad running toward me. There was fire falling down from the rafters. I remember that part."

Rachel put her hand over her mouth. Lucky was only half aware.

"Some of our horses were locked in their stalls, scream-ing, helpless. I got away from my dad and tried to run back to them. My shirt caught fire. Then there was no time. No more time. We barely got out before the roof collapsed." He looked over at her, finally letting the awful memory of that day engulf him like the flames themselves. "They airlifted me to a burn unit up north. And that's where I stayed for the rest of the summer."

Her eyes were wide, unblinking. Some of the color had drained from her cheeks. Maybe it was the look on his face that was affecting her now. Or maybe it was just the naked-ness of the words. There was no sugarcoating that story. Nothing that made it okay. The only thing that Lucky could take away from it, other than the guilt, was a powerful and unwavering compassion for animals. A deep sense of wanting to help the weakest and most vulnerable of them. Of trying to give back what he'd so carelessly taken that day. It was why he'd finally agreed to vet school. Even though his heart...his heart was somewhere else.

He smiled, and it felt forced on his mouth. But Lucky was used to forcing things, to getting through the best way he knew how.

"So," he said. "People have called me Lucky ever since. But my name is Jim."

Chapter Six

RACHEL ABSORBED THIS as she watched him from the back of the big palomino. *Jim.* It fit. It was sexy, a little old fashioned. But most of all, he just looked like a Jim, and she didn't think he'd ever been more attractive. And that was saying something. The image of him swaggering into the Graff that first time was tattooed onto her heart, whether she liked it or not.

But the way he'd opened up was what really made her stop and catch her breath. It wasn't just the story, which was enough to absorb on its own, but also the fact that she didn't think he told it often. The slight tilt to his head, the way his shoulders had stiffened when he'd recalled the memory, even the light in his eyes had dimmed noticeably.

"I'm so sorry," she said. "I'm so sorry that happened to you."

"I was a dumb kid. I understand that part. But the other stuff...it's harder to let go."

"What other stuff?"

His jaw muscles bunched and relaxed as he looked past her to the mountains in the distance. Maybe he was regretting telling her. Maybe she shouldn't have asked.

"Afterwards," he said, "I kind of became this live-wire. I never took things seriously, because then they couldn't be that painful." He shrugged. "It was a way to protect myself—I get that now. But it's why it took me so long to decide on graduate school, to finally commit. I used to have this vision of living my life in the most passionate way. Didn't matter if it was risky, as long as it was pushing the envelope. But not everyone is meant for that. At least my dad doesn't think so. And he's probably right."

Something inside her broke a little at that. And it might've been because it hit so close to home. It had taken her a long time to find the courage to reach for the stars, no matter how unattainable everyone else thought they were.

"You're not passionate about becoming a vet?" she asked. "That's not your dream?"

He looked at her, his gaze somber. "No."

"Then...why?"

"Because I'm still trying to prove to everyone that I'm more than just that screw-up kid. It's a way to grow up for good, I guess."

Nick shifted again, finding another clump of grass. Both horses grazed happily, undeterred by the bits in their mouths. "What would you most want to do then?" she asked. "If the sky was the limit."

"The entire sky?"

"The entire sky."

"If I could do anything..." he said, his voice suddenly thick. "I'd turn this place into a sanctuary for old and unwanted animals."

Rachel stared at him, a feeling of warmth blooming across her chest. Across her heart. "That's…that's…"

"Ridiculous?" It was like he expected a reaction that would require a defensive response. How many times had he defended this? And to whom? She could only guess, judging by the way he sat on his horse now, rigid and stony faced, that it had been a common theme at some point.

"Ridiculous?" she said. "*No*. In fact, it's maybe the best thing I've ever heard. Ever."

He smiled. "Then you're the only one."

"Why?"

"Well, for one, we'd have to update Sleigh Bell when my grandparents retire. Or at least part of Sleigh Bell. And financially that'd be risky. We'd have to add on to the barn, fine tune the pastures and turn-outs. Plus, running a non-profit is complicated." He shook his head. "It doesn't even matter; it's not going to happen anyway. I'm just saying I'd like to do it. Someday, maybe."

Rachel chewed on her cheek. "Could you do both? The sleigh rides *and* the sanctuary?"

"I think we could. In the end, I think each one would complement the other. But you'd have to have the man power for that, and, at the moment, it's just me, a few ranch hands, and my grandpa. I'd need to get my family on board. And my dad…"

Resting her hands on the saddle horn, she frowned, waiting for him to go on.

"To him," Lucky said, "it's like announcing I want to move to Hollywood and take acting lessons. Not that there's anything wrong with that, but, you know. It's a pipe dream as far as he's concerned."

"Maybe because he doesn't understand you can make a living that way. Maybe..." She had the overwhelming urge to finish her sentence, but also knew she was walking a delicate line. Listen without judgment or offer advice. He might not want any advice. Especially from someone he barely knew.

"Maybe what?"

"I don't know," she said. "Maybe you could explain it in a way that makes sense? Give him some examples of successful sanctuaries? I know of one in Oregon that's grown a ton in the last few years. I have a friend who lives out there and takes her fifth-grade class sometimes."

He smiled, but it was a tired looking smile. "I've already made up my mind. It's risky at best. Irresponsible at worst. It would take all my time, all my dedication. And, if it didn't work, we could lose this place, and that's not a gamble I'm willing to take."

She nodded, quiet for a minute. "What does the rest of your family think?" she finally asked. "As far as what will happen to the farm when Don and Loretta retire?"

"We need to talk about it. We haven't decided anything yet."

"So you're definitely going back to vet school?"

"I am. I'll have to make up some credits now, but yeah. It's the best thing."

She bit her tongue then. Because it really wasn't any of her business. She was here to take notes and tell their story.

That was it. And any affection she was starting to feel for this family was just something that she'd manufactured in her head. Because she'd always wanted a big family like this. A home like this. Somewhere to lay down roots.

She held his gaze underneath the December sunshine that was beginning to warm the day just a little. Nick lifted his head and sniffed noses with Pop Tart. The black and white horse let out a soft huff and shook her head, rattling her bridle.

"I think you'll make a wonderful vet," Rachel said.

And meant it.

Chapter Seven

RACHEL AND CHLOE walked down Main Street toward Grey's Saloon. The street lamps were just now winking on, the evergreen wreaths hanging from each pole looking festive in the frosty evening.

People walked past, sipping warm coffees and lugging shopping bags in their arms. Across the street, two small donkeys stood hitched to a beautiful red carriage, waiting patiently for their driver to get his passengers settled.

Rachel's gaze settled on the elegant green lettering on the side. *Sleigh Bell Farm, Marietta, Montana.* The donkey's harnesses were just as pretty—the rich, dark leather accented with shining silver bells. The little animals looked so cute in their fuzzy winter coats, both of them with matching red ribbons tied around their tails.

Her belly tightened before she realized the driver wasn't Lucky. A distinct disappointment washed over her, which was silly. What would she do if it was him, anyway? Run into his arms?

Sighing, she looked away. But Chloe noticed. Chloe *always* noticed.

"Want to tell me what's going on?"

"Nothing," Rachel said. "Why?"

"Well, for starters, you agreed to come out with me tonight, and that never happens."

"Maybe I got my knitting quota in for the month."

"You know I love my hats. And scarves. And mittens…"

Rachel laughed. "But?"

"*But* I do have to say, it's nice that you said yes for once. Which leads me to the obvious question…why?"

"Does there have to be a reason?"

They passed Sweet Pea Flowers, which had a display of chrysanthemums in their softly glowing window. The bright red arrangement sat in drifts of sparkling artificial snow. Twinkle lights hung over them, looking like a sky full of stars.

Chloe elbowed her. "There doesn't have to be a reason, but I know there *is* a reason. What's going on, Rach?"

Rachel buried her fists deeper inside the pockets of her down jacket and breathed into her scarf. Homemade, of course.

"I'm just…I don't know," she said. "Tired, I guess."

"Of?"

"Of trying to protect myself all the time. Of trying not to feel anything. That's a losing battle."

"And you're just now realizing this?"

"To be fair, it did work for a while."

Chloe smiled. "It did. And I got a few pairs of mittens out of that deal. But those last few guys were asshats, Rachel. You know most men aren't like that, right?"

"Yes, I know."

"But they also aren't all like the ones on your podcast either. Nobody's perfect."

"I know that too."

"Except…" Chloe hesitated.

"What?"

"Lucky Elliott might be close. At least from what you say."

At the mention of Lucky's name, Rachel warmed. "He's pretty amazing. I'm not gonna lie. He's…well, you've seen him. He's gorgeous."

"I *know*."

"And he's hard working. And smart and gifted and kind…"

"And perfect. Hate to say it."

She smiled. "No, he's not perfect. He's got his issues, just like everyone else."

"I'd stand in line for some of those."

"Me, too," Rachel said. "And that's the thing. I can't help seeing him as this knight in shining armor. I have to keep telling myself those don't exist. As much as I've always wanted them to."

Chloe put an arm around her. "I love how much of a romantic you are. You even give me hope for me.

"I'm too much of a romantic. I'm always getting disappointed."

"I know. But if you love, you're eventually going to get hurt. That's how it works. Better to have loved—"

"I know. Better to have loved an asshat, than to have never loved an asshat at all?"

Chloe laughed. "Okay, no. But you get the point. I'm just glad you're coming out with me. Maybe getting interested in guys again. And if not hottie Lucky, then someone else."

"Don't get too excited. I'm just craving a glass of wine."

"A glass of wine." Her friend winked and hooked her arm in hers. "Whatever you say, babe."

LUCKY SAT AT the heavy wood bar, scarred from a century of use—from cowboys drinking at it, breaking glasses on it, and maybe even a few heads over it. Grey's was the oldest building in Marietta, and if the Graff made a man feel like he was walking back in time when he passed through its doors, Grey's made him feel like he should be kicking off his boots and staying a while.

It was a saloon in every sense of the word. The only thing missing was the raucous piano music in the corner. Those tinny notes had long since been replaced by a jukebox, the warm whiskey with trendy local porters. It was the place to be on a Saturday night, but Lucky was in no mood for being out.

His cousin Patrick sat beside him, a white Stetson riding low over his eyes. He hadn't bothered taking off his worn Carhartt jacket, and he looked surly and tired. Lucky couldn't blame him. They'd met to talk about the farm, and if they could get the business through the holidays, which was iffy at best. Even with the miracle of the podcast advertising.

"I'm sorry all this is falling on your shoulders, man," Patrick said, picking up his beer to take a drink.

From across the room, someone smacked the pool balls and a group of people erupted in laughter. The song on the jukebox had switched to something Christmassy—something Garth Brooks and Trisha Yearwood.

"Everyone has their own stuff going on, Pat," Lucky said. "I know you all want to help."

"Whatever happens, you can count on me. You know that."

Patrick was a firefighter. He loved the farm just like everyone else, but like everyone else, he had a life to live that didn't necessarily include ranching.

"How are Grandma and Grandpa doing?" Patrick asked, picking at the label on his beer. "I was out last week, and he was talking about trying to work on the barn roof himself. Don't let him get up there with that knee."

"I won't if I can help it. But you know he does what he wants."

Across the room, the saloon doors swung open. Out of the corner of his eye, Lucky saw two women walk in, talking and laughing in soft tones. He didn't turn, but Patrick did, and his cousin ran a big hand down his handlebar mustache.

Lucky took a long swallow of his beer. He didn't look. He *would've* looked two weeks ago. He would've looked, while making his way over, with his best pickup line teetering on the edge of his tongue. But here, now, he could only picture one woman he really wanted to charm. And she was probably home with her cat. Because she'd told him as much the last time he'd seen her—sitting on Nick's back, her dark, silky hair blowing in front of her face. She was a homebody. She wasn't dating because she'd been hurt recently. And too many times before that. He got the distinct feeling the guys she was trying to steer clear of were just like him. Or guys she *thought* were like him.

Patrick's gaze shifted back to Lucky. "Why aren't you headed over there? You sick or something?"

Lucky laughed, and took another drink of his beer. "You wish. Less competition for you."

"Hey, I don't need any help."

"Keep telling yourself that."

Patrick grinned. They were the same age, and had always been close. It was Pat who'd sat beside his bed in the weeks after the fire. And Pat who'd defended Lucky when he got teased about the scars. His cousin had bloodied several kids' noses that fall. Until eventually, Lucky had learned to laugh with them. It hurt at first. But, after a while, he'd become desensitized to it.

Patrick glanced back across the saloon, and his easy smile faded. "Shit."

"What?" Lucky followed his cousin's gaze.

There, across the room, were two men. Loud, obnoxious. The kind who looked for trouble after a few beers and usually found it without a problem.

They were hassling a couple of women. And one of them...Lucky narrowed his eyes as recognition settled in. She pushed the man who'd just tried to touch her, with a low-key grit. A familiar tilt to her chin.

The blood in his veins cooled.

"They're—"

He was off the barstool before Patrick could finish his sentence. He pushed through the crowd without taking his eyes off Rachel.

He saw the guy reach for her again, and she scowled, shoving him away.

Her friend stepped up, looking pissed. The men were big. But, unfortunately for them, Lucky was bigger. And Patrick, who was bringing up the rear, dwarfed damn near everyone in Grey's.

The bar's music thumped in Lucky's ears, matching the pounding of his heart. The scent of cigarette smoke drifted in from outside when the door opened, bringing with it a cold gust of air. Everything smelled like cologne, smoke, and alcohol, and, all of a sudden, he felt close to losing it.

"Ladies," he said. "Everything okay?"

One of the men was sweaty and bald as a cue stick. The other was rangy and tallish, sporting a dirty baseball cap that looked vaguely 80s, but wasn't cool enough to be retro.

"They're fine, bud," the bald one said.

The other was busy sizing up Patrick. He didn't look nearly as lippy as his friend. "We were just talking."

"He wasn't asking you," Patrick said.

Rachel's gaze settled on Lucky then, and her mouth fell open. She was surprised to see him, that was obvious.

"We were just telling these assholes to take a long walk off a short pier," her friend said, her eyes sparkling. Lucky had a feeling, if he hadn't intervened, she would've had this situation wrapped up in a tidy little bow. Probably with these guys cradling what was left of their balls.

"Hey," Baldy said. "Just offering you a drink."

"And we said no. Emphatically." This from Rachel, who had her arms crossed over her lovely chest. Lucky's throat felt tight just looking at her.

With another wary glance, the two men finally turned and headed back to the bar, mumbling something as they went.

"Sorry about that," Lucky said. "I'm sure you could've handled it fine."

Rachel's friend smiled. "No, we can always use a little chivalry, can't we, Rach?"

"Chloe," Rachel's gaze never left his. "This is Lucky Elliot. And…"

"My cousin, Patrick," Lucky said.

"Nice to meet you, ladies." Patrick tipped his hat, and Chloe's red lips widened.

They all stood there as another Christmas song started playing on the jukebox. The music was loud. The voices around them louder. Lucky leaned toward Rachel and spoke into her ear, catching the scent of her faint perfume. "It's good to see you."

She looked up with those dark eyes. She had more makeup on tonight than she'd been wearing the other day, but he thought she might be blushing a little.

"It's good to see you too."

"Come here often?" He said this with a wink. It was

what he was best at. And it usually worked.

"You say that to all the girls?"

"Only the prettiest ones."

She smiled and looked away. And this time he was sure of it. Her cheeks, her throat were coloring before his eyes. A deep pink that suited her more than she'd ever know.

Chloe and Patrick had started chatting off to the side, and Rachel took a deep breath before looking up at him again. "To tell you the truth, I never come here."

"Why's that?"

"I don't go out very much. I probably told you that…"

He watched her, wanting to know more. Wanting those lips to keep moving. "Introvert?"

"Guilty as charged."

"So, why tonight?"

"I love my cat. Lucy. Lucille Ball."

Grinning, he leaned against the wall. "Go on."

"But Chloe pointed out that I'm getting a little too comfortable hanging out with her."

"So, Grey's."

"Chloe's idea."

He nodded again as a woman walked between them, muttering an apology.

"Chloe has good ideas," he said. "I'm glad you're here."

She looked around. "I'm having second thoughts though. I'd rather be…"

"What?"

"I don't know. Taking a walk or something. Enjoying the night air."

He wasn't usually attracted to quiet types. His very nature tended to scare them off. But there was something about her that seemed drawn to him, just like he was being drawn toward her. Maybe it was the alcohol talking, or the Christmas music, or the beauty of the stars he knew were scattered across the winter sky outside, that made him want to leave right then. To soak up exactly what she was suggesting.

"You know," he said, "we have a carriage down the block. Saturdays are busy during the holidays."

"I saw it. The donkeys are so cute."

"Dave and Betsy. This is their last night working, then we'll be putting them out to pasture. Literally."

She watched him, and he had trouble keeping his gaze off her mouth. She had a totally kissable mouth. Plump and expressive. And all of a sudden he couldn't remember where the hell he'd been going with the Dave and Betsy story.

"And it's just down the street?" she asked.

He blinked down at her. Oh, yeah. He'd been about to suggest taking a walk to see the donkeys. *Not* suggest kissing her, which was what he'd rather do instead.

"Want to meet them?" he asked. "They're pretty sweet. And they love baby carrots, which Pete probably has in his pocket."

She grinned. "The driver?"

"Yeah. He's worked at Sleigh Bell as long as I can remember."

"I'd love to."

He turned to Patrick and Chloe. "Would you two mind if we got out of here for a while? I was going to introduce

Rachel to Dave and Betsy."

Chloe looked confused.

"The donkeys we passed on the way here," Rachel said.

"Ahh," Chloe said. "You kids go ahead. Have fun!"

"You're sure?"

"Positive. This cowboy was about to buy me a drink anyway." She hooked her arm in Patrick's. "You guys have a nice walk. And text me if you get a ride home, Rach."

"Chloe…I'm not…"

"See ya, Luck," Patrick said. Then nodded at Rachel. "Ma'am."

After a second, the two of them wove their way toward the bar, lost to each other and the magic of waiting tequila shots.

"Well," Rachel said, staring after them. "That was fast."

Lucky laughed and touched the small of her back. Lightly, and only for a second, but long enough to feel an undeniable electricity spark at the tips of his fingers.

"Come on," he said. "Let's get out of here."

Chapter Eight

RACHEL WALKED ALONGSIDE Lucky, wanting to step closer, wondering what it would be like to have him put an arm around her and pull her into his warmth.

But then she remembered those kinds of thoughts, especially about Lucky Elliot, would lead straight to a broken heart. Or at least to a heart that might get kicked around a little, which was more than she was willing to risk.

So she walked along, tipping her head back to look at the stars twinkling so cheerfully in the night sky. Her breath puffed from her lips in silver clouds, and the tips of her ears were numb from the cold. But it felt good to be outside, away from the chaos and noise of the bar. But mostly, it felt good to be with Lucky. He made her laugh. He put her at ease. He made her want to do things like scratch elderly donkeys behind their ears, and catch snowflakes on her tongue. She guessed he probably had that effect on most people. There was something childlike about Lucky. And also something inherently wise. He was an anomaly.

He looked over. For some reason, she didn't trust herself to look back. She was too much in the moment. Too tethered to him emotionally, even though he might not be feeling the same. It was something she was painfully aware of.

"I meant what I said, you know," he said.

She shivered as a couple walked by holding hands. "About?"

"About being glad to see you tonight."

"Oh, yeah?"

"Yeah. And I wanted to tell you that I started listening to your podcast. From the first episode."

She did turn then. "You did?"

"You have a real talent for this, Rachel. The sound mixing, editing. All of it."

She grinned, and it felt like it might break her face in the chill of the night air. Like the farm for the Elliotts, her podcast was her baby. The creative bloom inside her heart that she nurtured on a daily basis, even though most people thought it was just a quirky hobby. She desperately wanted it to grow and thrive. She knew it was a card toss. But the dream was important to her just the same.

"That means so much," she said. "You really don't know *how* much."

He stopped and turned to her. There was a Salvation Army bell ringer on the corner, and people were slowing to put money in his red bucket. The bell chimed clear and lovely into the peaceful winter air.

"I might not know what it's like to have a podcast, or to work on something creative like that. But I know what it's like to have a dream that not everyone understands."

She looked up at him. He wore his sheepskin jacket tonight, the one he'd had on the first time she'd seen him, and the collar was pulled high around his neck. He had a western shirt on underneath—she could see a sliver of the blue plaid, and the color looked good on him. He was so handsome, that he made the pulse skip in her wrists. And he was standing there gazing down at her with a look in his eyes that said he did understand. He got it. And, if he got that, he got a crucial part of who she was. Of who she wanted to be.

"The sanctuary?" she asked.

"Yeah. Yeah, the sanctuary."

"You think about it? Even now?"

"Even now." He put his hands in his pockets. His broad shoulders were hunched a little, like he might be saying more than he'd planned. "Since meeting you, I've been thinking about it a lot, actually."

"You know I think it's an amazing idea."

He shook his head. "It wouldn't work. But what I'm saying is that I admire what you're doing. Your dream. You're all in, and I think that's pretty special."

Her face warmed. It felt so good to be acknowledged like this, that she didn't know how to respond at first. So many things were skipping across her mind. Including the thought of stepping close, standing on her tip toes, and giving him a kiss. A long, deep one. But she'd been thinking about that for a while, to be perfectly honest.

Licking her lips, she pulled in a breath. "I know you understand. I know how scary it is, Lucky. Especially with so much to lose. But you should think about it. Before you go back to school, before the student loan debt and all that comes with it. I just want you to know I don't think it's a crazy idea. Not by a long shot."

He was quiet at that. Standing there as people walked past, bundled up in their coats and scarves. Enjoying the kind of night Marietta was best at—when the holidays were close, and the beauty and charm of their small town was on full display.

"It's sweet," he said. "That you'd say that."

"I'm just being honest."

"I think you just want to save the animals of this county from my sub-par veterinary care."

She crossed her arms over her chest and looked up at him. "You're joking because you don't want to talk about the sanctuary. And I get it. But has anyone ever told you…like, *really* told you, how wonderful you'd be at it?"

His jaw muscles tensed, then relaxed. She really needed to shut it. It was none of her business.

He stared down at her, the warmth in his eyes cooling just a fraction. "Okay. Can I ask you a question?"

"Sure."

"Have you prepared yourself for your podcast failing? I'm not saying it will. I think it'll take off. But have you thought about it at all?"

"I think about it. But I don't dwell on it."

"And your mom? What does she think?"

It was like he'd turned her over to expose her tender underbelly. Her mom never thought anything would come of the podcasting. And as much as Rachel tried to pretend it didn't matter, that hurt. A lot.

"She thinks… Well, she doesn't believe I'll ever make a living from it."

His expression softened some. "And what about your friends?"

"They believe in it. Chloe did before I did."

"Because there's absolutely something to believe in. For me…it's just different. Everything begins and ends with my dad. His approval, or disapproval, has dictated my life for a long time. I have a lot to make up for, and I know it."

She nodded slowly. He was in pain. That might always be a part of who he was. "I understand," she said. "I just wish you could see what I see."

He stared down at her. And for the first time, she saw a spark behind his eyes, something that excited her for just a second. And then it was gone.

"You know," he said. "I'm not used to people pushing me much. Emotionally or otherwise."

She chewed the inside of her cheek. The bell continued ringing in the night air. People continued walking past, but she realized she hadn't noticed anything these last few minutes except for him. If he wasn't used to people pushing him, she wasn't used to pushing people. Yet, there was something about Lucky that made her want to step outside her comfort zone. She saw in him someone she wanted to be like. She sensed his passion, she'd seen that spark just now, even though he'd done his best to snuff it out first. The woman in her couldn't seem to look away.

"I don't know what's gotten into me," she said. "It's just that…"

He took a step closer then. She was hyper aware of his body, his warmth, his spicy, unique scent that seemed to permeate her very being. Her heartbeat slammed in her chest as he reached up and brushed her hair away from her cheek. His skin was rough, but his touch was soft as a dove's feather.

"It's just that what?" he said.

What she wanted to say, all the thoughts that had been bouncing around in her head just now, embarrassed her. He was going to think she was nuts or desperate. Or coming on to him. Which, maybe she wanted to. But Rachel had never in her life made the first move with a guy. Something that went all the way back to junior high and a deep fear of rejection.

"I like you," she said. And the words were out before she'd even known they'd been a possibility. Her face burned, because, even though what she'd said was innocent enough, it really meant much more than that. But she forced herself to plow on anyway. "And I want you to know how great I think you are. Not just with animals. That part is obvious. But with your grandparents, the farm. You're a really good guy, Lucky."

He moved closer. And she could actually feel the heat coming from his body. It didn't matter that they were standing on the sidewalk with the whole town watching. She wanted his mouth on hers. She wanted to plant her hands firmly against his chest, feeling the hardened points of his nipples through the western shirt that, let's face it, would look much better in a pile at her feet anyway.

He had no idea what he was doing to her. Or maybe he had every idea, and she was in for a load of trouble.

"If you keep talking to me like that, Rachel, I'm going to have to kiss you."

Her heart, which had been hammering before, jumped around like it was trying to find a way out. Her belly curled into a warm ball, and she could feel the pulse tapping behind her ears.

And then he was leaning close. Putting two gentle fingertips underneath her chin. Forcing her to maintain eye contact.

"You're just about the prettiest thing I've ever seen up close," he said. This time, his voice was gravelly and low. Nobody who was passing right then would've been able to hear. It was only for her. In this moment that was so public, and so intensely private at the same time.

She closed her eyes. She took a shaky breath. And she felt his warm, wet lips press against hers.

Everything fell away then. Anyone who might be watching, the chill of the air. The insistent ringing of the bell a few yards away. It was only Lucky. Maybe it had always been Lucky.

A strong arm wrapped around her lower back, bringing her close. Where she really wanted to be. Every single one of his sharp ridges and hard contours was a complete contradiction to the man himself. And the realization that she'd started falling for him long before this kiss on a dark, winter night, made the blood slow in her veins.

This was what she'd been trying to protect herself from.

This, right here. But, even as she formed the thought, she was powerless against it. It was as if she'd been waiting for him this whole time. His touch, his words, his very essence, which was as big as the Montana sky stretched out above them.

She felt his hand splay across her spine. Suddenly, she wanted it underneath her jacket, against her bare skin. She wanted his long, blocky fingers exploring her most tender places. She imagined he'd be good at that. He was good at everything else.

His tongue, warm and wet, flicked against her lips. It wasn't as much an invitation, as a glimpse of what he wanted. She longed for it too. So much it scared her. She shook from the outside in. Her knees were having trouble keeping her upright, and he seemed to sense it, holding her steady against his chest.

And then, slowly, he broke the kiss, leaving her aching. He stood there for a few precious seconds, breathing against her lips. Her eyes had been closed, and she opened them again reluctantly. He was looking down at her, his mouth wearing that crooked, confident smile she'd come to know as his and his alone. He could read her like a book. She couldn't hide a thing.

"I've been wanting to do that since that first day in the Graff," he said. "The first time I saw you."

Oh, God, oh, God... She could actually feel herself tumbling now. How was every woman in town not in love with this man? How did she even stand a chance? Rachel had never thought of herself as beautiful. She was attractive enough in a pinch, and she'd always been okay with that. Because not everyone could be Marilyn Monroe. But standing there next to a man who had the power to make her shiver just by looking at her, she was re-thinking all of it. She could only hope her heart could take this.

He loosened his hold on her, and she stepped back again. She was still shaking, but couldn't tell if it was from the kiss now or from the frosty air. Either way, she felt a profound loss by not being pressed up against him.

She reached up and touched her lips, which were still tingling. "Lucky," Her voice sounded funny. Like it was rolling off someone else's vocal chords. She hadn't even known she was going to say something until she'd opened her mouth.

He watched her steadily. "Uh oh. Is this the part where you tell me you just want to be friends?"

It was laughable, really. He had absolutely no idea how hard her heart was beating. How the delicate spot between her legs pulsed, even now.

She looked down at the buttons on his coat, just for something to do with her gaze that seemed to want to betray her every thought.

"I'm scared of this," she whispered.

He frowned. "You're scared of me?"

He hadn't heard her. But it was true—she *was* scared of him. She was scared of wanting him for her own. Because how could a man like Lucky ever truly belong to someone else? It seemed inconceivable that all that vibrancy could be harnessed into a traditional relationship. Everything Rachel had ever known about men said otherwise.

Regardless, she still wanted more. She'd always understood that about herself. Where her friends, like Chloe, could go out, have fun, and be with guys with no strings attached, Rachel couldn't. Maybe it was because of how her father had treated her mom. Whatever the reason, she knew she wouldn't be able to go much farther than this without breaking herself a little in the process. Right now, she needed to focus on her podcast. And, yeah. It was a little screwed up that she chose to live vicariously through other people's happily ever afters, but that was life. Everyone had their weird quirks.

Swallowing hard, she looked back up at him. His eyes were so dark, they didn't look blue anymore, so much as a deep gray. His jaw was clenched, his brows furrowed. There was an expression of worry on his face. For her. He was worried for her. And she fought against the sudden feeling of wanting to lay her head against his chest, and just let whatever was going to happen, happen. Screw the consequences.

But, then, she remembered the pain she'd felt the last time she'd let go. She remembered her mother's pain too. She really had everything she needed anyway. She had her podcast. She had her cat. She had Chloe and Bob and a small group of friends who loved her. That was enough love for now. It really was.

"I'm not scared of you," she said. "I'm scared of this. Of getting in over my head."

He licked his lips, and her eyes were automatically drawn to his mouth. That mouth. She pictured it on her breast, moving, sucking. Which was precisely the problem. She couldn't *not* picture these things, which made her feel completely out of control. And she was all about control.

"It was only a kiss, Rachel. I'd never hurt you."

She looked up at him. And there it was. *Only a kiss...* "I know you wouldn't," she said. "Intentionally. But you're also headed back to school. And you've got so much on your plate right now. Starting something isn't smart. For you or for me."

"Ahh. You're letting me down easy."

"I'm letting *me* down easy."

He smiled. "I really wouldn't, you know. Hurt you."

"All guys say that. And then they do."

"I'm not all guys."

"I know. That's what I'm afraid of."

He held his hand out, and she grabbed it, grateful for the solidness he offered.

"Come on," he said. "Let's go meet the donkeys."

They fell into step beside each other, breathing in the scent of warm baked goods coming from the Java Café.

In the distance, she could see the carriage parked in front of Big Z Hardware and Lumber, which was decked out in multi-colored lights and a blow-up snowman out front. The carriage would be replaced by the antique sleigh soon, if the forecast had anything to say about it. There was a couple climbing down the narrow steps, and a small family waiting to get in. The driver, an older man wearing a heavy jacket, Wranglers, and boots, glanced over as they approached. He waved, calling them over.

Looking both ways, they headed across the street.

"Just in time," the driver said. "I was just headed out. Coming to check on them?"

"I have someone who wanted to say hello," Lucky said, giving the other man a slap on the back. "Rachel, this is Pete. Pete, this is Rachel. She's the podcaster I was telling you about."

She held out her hand. "Nice to meet you, Pete."

"Likewise, ma'am."

He had warm hazel eyes and a thick, graying mustache. A Montana cowboy through and through. The kind who held the door open for you in the rain and went to church on Sundays. Tough and grizzled. Plain and kind.

He turned to the family behind him. "You folks go ahead and climb on. We'll get going in just a minute. There's a blanket to cozy up with and hot chocolate in the thermos. The cups and napkins are underneath the seat there."

The little girl, who looked five or so, grinned from ear to ear.

Pete's weathered gaze settled on Lucky, and he nodded toward the donkeys. "These guys are tired tonight, boss."

Lucky reached out and stroked one of the donkey's noses so tenderly that Rachel felt a lump rise in her throat. The animals stood quietly in their festive harnesses and ribbons, doing what was asked of them. Their whole lives had been in service to their human friends, and something about that touched her to the core.

She couldn't see their eyes from where she stood, because of the big, square blinders, but their ears rotated in her direction. Listening to her, reading her.

"Which one is Dave, and which is Betsy?" she asked.

Lucky rubbed the lighter gray one on the cheek until the animal leaned into him. "This is Dave," he said. "And that's Betsy. When she came to us, I was just a kid."

"She'd been abused," Pete said. "But with Lucky's help, she healed. He won't say it, but he stayed with her twenty-four hours a day. Loretta couldn't get him to come inside to eat or sleep. He just sat in her stall. Took days, but he was the very first one she let close."

"If people are patient enough, gentle enough," Lucky said, "anyone can do it."

"But that's the thing—most people aren't. We always knew you were special. That you'd do something with it someday."

Rachel reached out and rubbed Dave behind his giant ears. So soft. Like rabbit's fur. "He'll be a great vet," she said. But there was a part of her, a small, insistent part, that was sad he wasn't following his heart.

Lucky's phone rang from his pocket, startling the donkeys.

Muttering an apology, he stepped away and answered it.

"What?" he said. "When?"

Rachel waited, a feeling of dread settling into her stomach. It could be anything. But the way he stood, the sound of his voice…

"I'll be right there," he said, and hung up.

He looked over at Rachel.

"Grandpa fell," he said. "I'm sorry. I need to get home."

Chapter Nine

L UCKY STOOD THERE, almost frozen for a minute, until Rachel stepped forward.

"What?" she said, putting her hand on his arm. "What happened?"

He raked a hand through his hair. "He was putting up Christmas lights. I told him not to. I told him I'd do it this weekend."

"Oh, no."

"I can cancel this last run, Lucky," Pete said. "Do you need me to come with you?"

"It's okay. You stay here and finish out the night. I don't want to disappoint these folks." Right as he said it, the little girl squealed when Betsy shook her head, letting some slobber fly.

"Do you want me to ride along?" Rachel asked. "If you need to take him to the hospital, I can stay with Loretta."

The simple offer made something inside him tighten. His grandparents were getting older, more frail by the day. He was pissed at himself for not putting the lights up earlier. Guilt, warm and thick, crept over him like an unwanted blanket.

He opened his mouth to argue, to tell her she didn't have to. But the look on her face made him stop. Even though she didn't know his grandparents well, he knew she felt a connection with them. She wanted to come. To help in some way. That was obvious.

"Okay," he said. "Thank you."

She smiled. And reached for his hand.

THEY SPENT THE drive out to the farm in relative silence. Lucky had called his grandma again, but she hadn't picked up. He was trying to keep his mind from going to the worst places—mostly how they seemed to have dodged a bullet this time, but what about next time? Sleigh Bell was getting to be too much for them. At this point, he had no idea how willingly they'd end up walking away.

Rachel looked over at him as they passed shadowy farms in the distance. The stars stretched overhead, making the night seem infinite. The heater blew gamely from the vents in the dash, but wasn't doing much to warm him.

"You okay?" she asked.

He nodded, but didn't look back. For some reason, he felt too exposed. Too vulnerable. He wasn't used to talking when his feelings were this close to the surface. If anyone else would've asked to come tonight, he would've said no. But her presence was an undeniable comfort right then. And he was still grappling with how that had come to be.

"I'm alright," he said. "Just worried. A broken bone at

this age…"

She reached over and put a hand on his thigh. "I know."

"I've always," He licked his lips, which were suddenly dry. "I guess I've never told anyone this because it makes me feel guilty saying it out loud."

"What?"

Clenching his jaw, he paused for a few seconds before answering. "I've always felt closer to my grandparents than my parents. I mean, my brothers, cousins, and I were basically raised on the farm. My dad was gone a lot. My mom wasn't much of a nurturer. My grandmother did most of that. And I wanted to be just like my grandpa. Just like him."

"That doesn't surprise me. He's pretty great."

He rubbed his thumbs over the worn leather of the steering wheel. "He's getting old. They both are, and truthfully, I'm struggling with that. When I was a kid, there was nothing they couldn't do. And now…"

Headlights approached and flashed in his eyes. He squinted as the lonely car passed on the highway.

"And now, everything you know is changing," she said softly.

"Yeah," he said. "That."

"It's normal, Lucky. Your life is moving in a different direction, and so is theirs."

She was right. His life was moving somewhere other than the farm, and he wasn't entirely sure he was happy about that. The ache in his chest said he wasn't. The sudden tightness in his throat. He wanted Sleigh Bell to live on. To be the legacy his grandparents had spent their lives building. And what would happen to it if he left? He'd seen family businesses taken over by strangers. Sometimes it worked out, but most of the time, the inherent magic was lost somewhere in the transfer. It's just how it was. Everything had a lifespan. Was Sleigh Bell nearing the end of its own?

He glanced over at Rachel. The gentle weight of her hand on his thigh was something he could get used to.

"I'm glad you came," he said.

"I'm glad, too."

He watched her for a second longer, then put his blinker on for Sleigh Bell's long, dirt drive. A few horses stood grazing near the fence line, nothing but silhouettes in the still of the night.

He turned the truck onto the driveway, and the loose gravel crunched underneath the tires. Soon, this would all be covered in snow. But, tonight, it was a clear, dry pathway to the old house, which stood so regally in the distance, waiting for her visitors.

The lights were on in the downstairs windows, illuminating the wraparound front porch. There was an overturned ladder by the steps, and a string of red and green twinkle lights in a discarded coil on the ground. They were eerily lit, as if they'd been dropped on the spot, which, of course, they had been, and the sight made Lucky's skin prickle.

"It's a miracle it wasn't worse," Rachel said.

He pulled up to the house and jammed the truck into park. "I hope so. We'll see."

Together, they got out and climbed the steps to the front

door. Lucky opened it with a heavy feeling in the pit of his stomach.

"Grandma? Grandpa?"

"We're in here, honey," his grandmother called, her voice an octave higher than normal.

Stitch came running, and Lucky bent to give him a quick pat before heading into the kitchen.

There, sitting on one of the old dining room chairs, was his grandpa. There was blood all over his white thermal shirt, and he was pressing a towel to his head.

"Shit," Lucky muttered, crossing the room in a few long strides.

Stitch, knowing something was wrong, trotted over and sat at his master's feet with a whine.

Lucky's grandma stood wringing her hands and looking a little sick. She was a strong lady, had seen more injuries on this farm than he cared to admit, including his own massive burns. But she seemed fragile now, and every bit her age, which he wasn't used to.

Before Lucky could say anything, Rachel appeared and wrapped an arm around her shoulders.

"Here, Loretta," she said gently. "Let's sit down, okay?"

He knelt beside his grandfather on one knee. "What happened?"

"I know you said to wait on those lights, but I wanted your grandma to be able to see them through the kitchen window."

He looked so much older sitting there at the kitchen table, trying not to make a mess on the floor. It wasn't just the blood or the embarrassed expression on his deeply lined face.

It was his entire demeanor. He looked smaller somehow.

"Can I see your head?" Lucky asked.

Stitch whined again and lay down with his head on his paws.

His grandfather winced before taking the towel away. The gash had bled a ton, and the edges were turning a bluish-violet color Lucky didn't like the look of.

"You need to go to the hospital," he said. "I think you'll need stitches, and you might have a concussion."

"Oh, it's not that bad. I'll be okay."

"Donald." This from his grandmother. "You're going."

He shook his head. "I've taken so many spills. This isn't any different." But the tremor in his voice made Lucky think he knew this *was* different. Maybe not the wound itself. But what the wound meant.

His grandma got up and came over to where her husband sat. He looked up and smiled. She touched his cheek in a way that made Lucky wonder what one of them would ever do without the other. It was unfathomable imagining them apart.

"It's hard, sweetheart," she said. "Life is full of choices we don't want to make. Or that we think we're not ready to make. But it's going to be just fine."

It was obvious she wasn't talking about the hospital anymore. And the knowledge was like a punch to the gut. Something finite and cold. Something Lucky was going to have to face, one way or another.

His grandfather looked over at him then. "Son, will you drive your grandma and me to the hospital? We'd sure appreciate it."

Chapter Ten

R ACHEL SAT BESIDE Lucky in the waiting room of Marietta General's small emergency room. There were only two other people waiting to be seen. A little boy with stomach pain, who was curled up on his dad's lap, and a cowboy who looked like he'd picked a fight with someone bigger.

As far as emergency rooms went, this one was surprisingly pleasant—painted in warm shades of yellow and bathed in soft overhead lighting. There was a Christmas tree standing by the front desk, trimmed with paper snowflakes made by the hospital's pediatric patients. Christmas music played through the overhead speakers, and the whole place smelled like coffee and freshly waxed floors.

Beside her, Lucky flipped through a magazine. Don and Loretta had been taken back about an hour ago. He was getting some stitches and a CT scan just to be sure. The nurse who'd talked to them had been very reassuring, but Lucky still wore a deep furrow between his brows.

Rachel touched his knee, coaxing his gaze up from the magazine—something with a horse on the cover.

"Do you want some coffee?" she asked.

He shook his head, looking at her as if she'd just materialized from thin air. "Sorry I've been quiet. Just processing, I guess."

"You don't have to be sorry."

"Thanks for coming. You've been...amazing." The look on his face warmed then. "Are you sure you don't want a ride home, though? It might be a while before he gets discharged."

"If you're okay with me staying, I'm good. I don't want to leave you."

Overhead, a doctor was being paged. A couple of nurses came running, clutching the floppy stethoscopes around their necks.

Lucky shifted in his seat. After a minute or two, he rubbed a hand over his stubbled jaw.

"I don't like hospitals much," he said.

Her heartbeat slowed in her chest. *Of course.* Of course he didn't like hospitals.

Reading the look on her face, he shook his head. "It's alright. It's just certain smells that bring it back. Some sounds. The elevators dinging and things like that. Weird, huh?"

"It's not weird at all." She twisted her hands in her lap, thinking of the little boy in that hospital bed all those years ago. "It must've been so painful. I can't even imagine."

He clenched his jaw. He was taking a moment. Being here must be worse than he let on.

"Burns are hard," he said. "I had to take these baths so they could peel away the skin." There was a distant look in his eyes, and he paused before going on. "The fire, the aftermath, it was what it was. But honestly, that's one thing about veterinary medicine that doesn't thrill me. There's a lot of urgency, late night calls. Life and death situations. I know I'll get over it, but I've had enough of that kind of urgency to last a lifetime."

She wondered if she should say what she was thinking. Reminding herself it was none of her business. But then saying it anyway. "Do you *want* to get over it?"

He looked over at her.

"That's not what I mean," she said quickly. "I mean…would it be better if you didn't have to keep opening those wounds?"

"It's all part of the job."

"Well, yeah. It's all part of being a vet. I'm just saying…"

"You're just saying I wouldn't have to deal with that stuff as much running a sanctuary."

"No…yes. Kind of."

He smiled. "You're a terrible liar."

"I know. I can't seem to let it go. But it's only because I think you were born to do it."

He took her hand and pulled it into his lap. She was pretty sure he didn't mean for it to turn her on. Since they were sitting in the middle of an emergency room. But she had to concentrate on the words that were coming out of his mouth, instead of the feel of his rough, sexy fingertips on the backs of her knuckles.

"I like hearing you say those things," he said. "Even though I don't think the sanctuary would work, I still like thinking about it. Imagining what it would be like."

"You do?"

"Yeah"

She waited, glimpsing a crack in his perfectly constructed armor. And seeing some light shine through.

"I've been thinking how it would be financially possible," he continued. "I'd have to have a partner. Or two…"

She nodded slowly.

"Out of all my brothers and cousins," he said, "Patrick would probably be the one to go in on something like this. He loves the farm. And he knows we'd have to take it in a different direction in order to keep it going."

"Have you mentioned it to him?"

"In a roundabout way."

"What'd he say?"

"I didn't give him a chance to say anything. If I go to vet school, I can help my grandparents for a while. Hire on more help. And then we'll just figure it out as it comes."

"But what about you, Lucky?"

"What about me?"

"What about doing what makes you happy?"

He squeezed her hand, but the look on his face said he was done talking about it. "Too many people are counting on me right now. I can't afford to mess this up. I don't know what it would do to my grandparents if we lost the farm. And it could happen, Rachel. Taking on more animals and scaling back on the sleigh ride business, even a little, could tip the scales in a way we could never recover from."

"Or it might be the best thing you ever did."

He watched her.

"Don and Loretta took a big chance taking over that place, didn't they?"

He nodded.

"But it worked. They built a life, they built a business. And they raised a family there. None of that would've happened if they hadn't taken that chance."

"No, it wouldn't have. But things aren't as magical as that first kiss story, Rachel. There were really hard times growing up. They glossed over those parts for you."

"I know…"

A nurse came in and called the cowboy's name from across the room. Wilbur. His name was Wilbur. He stood, tall as a glass of water, and tilted his head back to pinch the bridge of his nose.

They watched him follow the nurse through the swinging doors. Then Rachel turned to Lucky again.

"Can I ask you one more thing?"

"Shoot."

"Have you talked to your grandparents about the sanctuary?"

He frowned. "No. Not really."

"Why?"

"Because they'd assume that's what I wanted. And then they'd want it for me. I know they're going to leave the land to me, my brothers, and cousins—my family agreed on that years ago. But the business side will be mine. They trust me, and I need to do the most responsible thing with it."

"But maybe it's what they'd want too. Just maybe."

He didn't smile, didn't say something light, like she'd come to expect. Instead, a solemn expression crept over his features. "Why do you believe in me like this?"

She contemplating that for a second. She couldn't understand why he didn't see what she did. It was like convincing someone the sun was warm, or that water froze in the winter.

"Why *don't* you believe in yourself, Lucky?"

He sat there, quiet, as the hospital sounds hummed around them. As they waited for Don to be discharged, and for life to resume its relentless trek forward.

He didn't answer. Maybe because he didn't have an answer that fit.

Chapter Eleven

RACHEL TOOK HER electric blue headset off and pushed the microphone away. She sat there for a minute fighting the ache in her throat, then gave up and let the tears come in earnest.

Wiping them away, she sat back in the office chair she'd gotten at a garage sale last spring, and pulled her knees up to her chest. Her pajama bottoms smelled like lavender, her favorite. The scent was comforting—it reminded her of growing up in her mother's house. But it also reminded her of practical things, like learning how to do the laundry at nine because she'd had to grow up fast, without a dad around. And the emotional punch that followed was unexpected.

Recording Don and Loretta's first kiss episode had dredged up a lot of feelings for her. Ones she'd seen coming. And ones she hadn't. She knew some of that had to do with the Elliott family and what they represented for her as an only child of parents who'd only been together in theory. She admired their stability, their togetherness. The little girl in her would probably never stop longing for a whole family. For two parents and two sets of grandparents. It was a void she knew would never be completely filled, no matter how many lovely first kiss stories she told. No matter how many couples she grew to care about.

Lucy meowed at her feet, and Rachel shifted and patted her lap. The little cat jumped up and immediately began a throaty purr. A big sound for such a tiny creature.

Smiling, she stroked the soft fur, the fluffy tail. Then looked out the window at the steely gray clouds overhead, and sighed. Part of the emotions today had to do with Lucky's family. The other part had to do with Lucky himself.

It had been a little less than a week since the night Don had fallen off the ladder. Since she and Lucky had shared that steamy kiss on Main Street. But she batted away those particular butterflies before they could properly take flight. Just because they'd kissed didn't mean anything else was going to happen. In fact, she'd barely heard from him since last Saturday.

He was understandably swamped—trying to take care of the farm, figuring out his grandparents' situation, and dealing with their new reality. He'd texted a few times, but that was all. And she got it. She really did. He'd be going back to school soon anyway. But, no matter how many times she told herself this was life in all its messiness and unpredictability, it still didn't keep her heart from hurting.

Her gaze shifted back to her computer. She'd spend tonight fine-tuning; editing and polishing up the sound, and then she'd upload the episode in the morning. She was excited for the coverage it would give Sleigh Bell. She'd hit three thousand subscribers just last night, and had texted

Lucky to let him know. She wasn't sure why he'd been the first person she'd wanted to tell, but he had been. And he'd texted back saying he was proud of her.

She guessed she could try and explain her feelings away all she wanted to, but, deep down, she felt a connection to him that went beyond just physical attraction. She sensed in Lucky a dreamer, like she was. Someone who wanted to reach for something big and hang on to it. As tightly as his arms would allow.

Watching a few snowflakes swirl outside the window, she startled when the doorbell rang. She pushed Lucy off her lap, making her squeak in protest.

"I bet that's your Aunt Chloe."

The cat blinked up at her indignantly.

"I know. But you love your Aunt Chloe."

Lucy stalked toward her little bed, feathers ruffled.

Getting up, Rachel put her slippers on. Chloe said she might stop by this afternoon before their shift. She'd borrowed a jacket of Rachel's, since it was doing nothing in her closet except gathering dust. Somebody might as well be putting it to use.

It was good she'd made it over early. It was supposed to dump soon. Luckily, Rachel lived close enough to the Graff that she could walk. If not, she could always ask Bob for a ride, since he practically drove a snowplow.

She headed into the living room, her bunny slippers scraping over the hardwood floor. Looking through the peephole, she frowned when she saw it wasn't Chloe, but someone holding a package instead.

She unlocked the deadbolt and opened the door. "Hi, there."

A teenage girl looked up. Her glasses were spattered with snowflakes, forcing her to squint through them. "Rachel O'Rourke?"

"That's me."

"I'm Daisy from the Copper Mountain Gingerbread and Dessert Factory. We have a custom cookie order for you."

Rachel felt her mouth stretch into a ridiculous smile. She'd never gotten anything custom before. Except maybe a birthday cake. "Really?"

The girl nodded, shivering. "Yup." She handed over a pink bakery box. "Enjoy."

Rachel grabbed a tip from her purse. "Here you go," she said. "Thank you." She stepped back inside and closed the door. She had no idea who could've sent her cookies. Yet, here she was. Holding a box that smelled like the sugar and vanilla gods had blessed it before sending it along with a teenage junk food angel name Daisy.

She walked into the kitchen and set the box on the table. They were probably from Chloe. She did sweet things like this sometimes. Probably because she felt sorry for Rachel, who she thought didn't have a life. Which, she *did*. She did have a life. It was just full of lots of knitting. And stuff.

Lucy weaved around her ankles. Rachel looked down at her. "They're probably from Chloe. Nice, huh?"

Lucy looked up and meowed. It was impossible to tell what her opinion was.

Rachel steeled her heart for absolutely no reason, because

it didn't really matter who they were from, only that someone cared enough to send them, and opened the lid.

There, in delicate white tissue paper, sat two large cookies. They were in the shape of donkeys, and were the most beautifully decorated cookies Rachel thought she'd ever seen. But these weren't just any donkeys. They were Sleigh Bell donkeys. They wore harnesses in black frosting with tiny red ribbons in their tails.

Gasping, she reached for a simple, white card tucked underneath the tissue paper and opened it.

> *In honor of the first kiss story that started it all. Thank you for telling it. Love, Dave and Betsy.*

Rachel laughed at the same time tears welled in her eyes. *Lucky.* Okay. So, she'd been hoping he'd sent them. Because getting custom-made cookies was maybe the most romantic thing ever.

She picked one up. They were almost too pretty to eat. But she bit off one of the donkey's ears anyway, sending her into a near buttergasm.

"Oh. My. God."

Lucy stared up at her.

"I know. They're just…just…"

Lucy meowed.

"Yes. That."

Rachel looked out the window to where the snow was beginning to stick. Soon, it'd be a winter wonderland. She took another bite of cookie, savoring its sweetness. Savoring the warm feeling unfurling inside her chest. This felt close to perfect. But she knew perfection didn't exist.

The first needles of fear prickled her heart. And she wondered how long it would be until it broke in two.

LUCKY PULLED THE collar of his jacket high around his neck and dug his hands into his pockets. It had snowed all night, and trudging through the thick blanket of it on the sidewalk was a chore. Even so, people passed him, undeterred by the weather. In fact, the locals seemed to revel in it. Good boots, a warm jacket, and a pair of gloves, and you were good to go. And if you were a true Mariettan, it didn't stop you from shopping either. Christmas was right around the corner, and the evidence was everywhere: lit trees, mistletoe, candy canes, holiday music. There was even a newly erected snowman in front of the fire station, where he was headed now.

Slowing, he looked both ways to cross the street, but stopped when he heard his name.

"Lucky! Lucky Elliott!"

He turned to see Sage Carrigan in front of Copper Mountain Chocolate Shop, looking pretty as usual. Her red hair was up today, and she wore a festive green turtleneck that complimented her fair skin. She was shaking out a rug, while strategically holding the door open with her hip.

He waved. "Hey, Sage!"

"I heard the episode this morning," she called out. "It was great! If you see Rachel, tell her what an amazing job she's doing, okay?"

He smiled. He'd listened too. So had half the people he knew. He'd gotten at least a dozen texts this morning, and Sleigh Bell's phone was ringing off the hook.

But the thing that made him most happy was how Rachel's podcast seemed to be taking off. Folks connected with it, because almost everyone had a first kiss story of their own. Most people could relate. And everyone liked a happily ever after. He wanted this for Rachel—for her to realize her dream. He couldn't think of anyone more deserving.

He waved again. "I'll tell her! Thanks for listening!"

Flashing a smile, Sage headed back inside.

Lucky stepped off the curb toward the station. The garage door was open, and a couple of firefighters were polishing an engine inside. It gleamed, its chrome wheels reflecting the sun, which was trying its best to peek through the clouds overhead.

A fat Australian Cattle Dog waddled out to meet him.

"Hey, there," Lucky said, bending to give it a pat. "You haven't missed many meals, have you boy?"

Patrick walked around the firetruck's grill, wiping it down with a rag. "She's a girl. And she says you can stick it."

Lucky knelt in the snow to rub the dog's ears, earning a happy wiggle and a few licks on the chin. "I'm sorry," he said. "Of course, you're a girl. Of course, you are."

Patrick tossed the rag into a bucket, looking amused. "I think she forgives you. And she might be in love. You and animals, man. Be careful, or she'll follow you home."

"I've got Stitch in my truck. So unless we want cattle dog-Stitch mixes, that'd be a hard pass."

Patrick laughed and leaned against the truck, looking fit in his navy blue slacks and fleece pullover with the fire department insignia on the chest.

"What are you doing here?" he asked. "I thought we were meeting for a beer later."

"We are, but you said you wanted to tell me something, and I was in town to pick up a few things for grandpa anyway. So I thought I'd stop by."

Squinting into the sunshine, Patrick nodded. "Okay. Well, I'll just tell you now, then. We can talk about the details tonight."

Lucky straightened, and the dog waddled back into the garage toward a cushy pink bed.

"What details?" Lucky asked. "What's going on?"

Patrick stuck his hands in his pockets and sighed, his breath crystalizing on the morning air. "I listened to the podcast this morning."

"Oh, yeah?"

"Yeah."

"What'd you think?"

"I thought it was great," Patrick said. "Mostly. Mostly, it was great."

"Okay…"

His cousin frowned. "Are you still planning on going back to vet school, Lucky?"

"That's," Lucky paused, sensing some kind of battle of wills. But over what, he wasn't sure yet. "That's the plan."

"Even though you don't want to."

"What? Where'd you get that from?"

"The clip of your interview this morning. You were talking about vet school and being able to help with the farm that way. We all know you want to send money back to Grandma and Grandpa. But we've also accepted something by now that you haven't."

He stiffened. "And what's that?"

"No amount of money you send back is going to save this farm. Not in its current state. Don't you think, if that was the case, we'd all be doing the same?"

He felt the muscles across his shoulders tense. "It's the only solution," he said flatly. "The only thing that's going to work for now. I never said it'd be for the long haul. Obviously, we'll have to reevaluate in a few years. But for now…"

"What's going to work for now, is having someone in the family *there*. On the farm. Working it. Hiring anyone else on is problematic for a shit-ton of reasons. Not to mention, good luck finding someone Grandpa trusts enough."

Lucky rolled his head from side to side. His temples were beginning to throb. A big pickup passed, and he waited for its rumbling engine to fade before answering his cousin.

"I know," he finally said. "I know that. But what else do we do? Nobody is stepping up."

Patrick crossed his arms over his chest. "How about you?"

Lucky stared at him. "What?"

"You heard me."

"What the hell are you talking about?"

"I know about the sanctuary idea, cousin."

"I don't…"

"You do. I talked to Rachel's friend the other night. Remember Chloe?"

He did remember. An attractive blonde. But he'd been so focused on Rachel, he didn't remember much else. "You talked to her?" He was still having trouble wrapping his head around this conversation, which had come out of left field.

"That night at Grey's," Patrick continued. "When you and Rachel left, Chloe and I hung out. For a while, actually."

"Go on."

"Well, after the second drink, we started talking about you guys."

"Oh, holy hell."

"No, it's okay. It really is. Because we figured a few things out."

"I don't want to know."

"You and Rachel should date," Patrick went on, completely ignoring him. "You have a lot in common."

Lucky raised his brows.

"Also, Chloe told me Rachel told her that you were thinking of starting up an animal sanctuary. Of converting Sleigh Bell?"

"*No.* No, I'm not thinking of doing it. It crossed my mind, that's all."

"Well, I think it should've done more than cross it, Lucky. It's a great idea."

Lucky shoved his hands further into his pockets and looked out at the jagged, white mountains in the distance. The sanctuary had always been such an abstract concept, he'd never allowed it to gain a foothold in his brain. Not really. Lucky was his own worst enemy, coming up with excuse after excuse why it wouldn't work.

But he had to admit that something had shifted the day he'd told Rachel about it. She'd listened quietly, validating him in a way that he'd never validated himself. He'd shut her down, of course. But the idea had been gnawing at him ever since. It had made a hole big enough that he couldn't find the right words to respond to his cousin now. Words of any kind had deserted him.

"Just admit it," Patrick said.

"There's nothing to admit. Even if I wanted to, there are too many variables. The family would have to agree. And in order to agree, they'd have to be okay with the risk. And I'm not going there, man."

"The fact is, you don't know *what* the family would agree to, because you haven't bothered asking."

Lucky shook his head. "It's just easier this way. It makes the most sense."

"What does? Putting a Band-Aid on the problem? Eventually, we're going to have to figure out what's next for Sleigh Bell. A sanctuary, with you running it, would be the best way to honor the farm. You really think when Grandma and Grampa got married, they pictured handing it over to some stranger when they retired? No. No way. They'd want this for you. For all of us."

Lucky laced his hands behind his head. The air was biting cold, but he barely noticed. "Even if I could do it, even if it made it through Dad, which, by the way, he'd *never* go for ...I couldn't do it alone. Not with the sleigh ride business, too."

"How about a partner then?"

He frowned. "What?"

"I'm in, Lucky. I have some money put away. I'd invest in this."

Something wrapped itself around Lucky's heart and squeezed. Ever since the day he'd come home from that burn unit all those years ago, he'd been afraid of people trusting him again. Really trusting him. Because letting them down wasn't an option anymore.

"You have no idea what that means to me," he said, his voice thick. He cleared his throat. "But I can't."

"Why not?"

"It's more than just the money. It would be an entire sanctuary. *And* the business. That's biting off more than I could chew, and I know it."

"When I said I'd help, I didn't just mean by writing you a check."

Lucky watched his cousin steadily, his pulse tapping in his neck.

"I meant I'm all in," Patrick said. "I'll be your partner."

It took a few seconds for that to sink in. A few seconds of standing there in the snow, with cars driving by in the slush.

"Why?" he finally asked.

"Why not? I keep telling you, this makes sense. In every way, it makes sense. I can still be a firefighter. I'm lucky because I have flexible hours here. You can still run the sleigh ride business. And together, we can run the sanctuary. The best of both worlds. A way the farm can reinvent itself in order to survive long term. A way to help our community *and* animals."

Lucky smiled.

"I know a thing or two about ranching, dude," Patrick said. "You'd be pretty hard pressed to find a better partner."

"I'm tempted," he said slowly. "And I wouldn't have thought that was possible before today. But…"

"But, what?"

He watched his cousin, but wasn't really seeing him. He could almost smell the charred hair from that day. Could smell his own burning skin and hear the sound of his gelding screaming from his stall. The memories were that thick. And it was too much. All of it.

"But I've spent my life trying to prove myself to this family. Trying to prove that I'm better than what I did."

Patrick stepped forward, his dark brows furrowed. "Why? Because, as a kid, you made a mistake?"

"I was old enough to know better. Almost eleven, for Christ's sake. At eleven, Jake was on his first steer. And, if I forgot, Dad was always there to remind me."

"You're not Jake, Lucky. And you can't be paying for this your entire life. You need to try and forget about it."

"I can't forget about it," he said.

"Aww, shit," Patrick mumbled, his gaze flickering to Lucky's midsection where the scars were hidden underneath his clothing. "I'm sorry, man. But you have to find a way to move forward. You're acting like starting up a sanctuary is some kind of long shot. It's not. People do it every day and succeed. You could, too. You just have to take a leap of faith to get there."

Lucky gritted his teeth. He'd been ready to go back to school. Resigned to it. He knew he'd be a good vet, and it was an honorable profession—something that'd make his parents proud. Really, that's all he'd ever wanted.

Until he met Rachel. Telling her about the sanctuary had opened something inside him that he was having trouble closing off. She'd seen it. And, now, so did Patrick, who was doing his best to pry it open the rest of the way.

"What are you thinking?" Patrick asked. "Talk to me."

"I'm thinking I wouldn't even know where to begin."

"Just take some time to think about it. *Really* think about it. Because once you go back to school, once you commit to that, it's gonna be really hard to walk away. To figure out what you truly want out of life."

The winter sun settled its rays on Lucky's shoulders, warming him. The icicles hanging from the fire department gutters sparkled like fine crystals in the morning light.

He had no idea what he was going to do. When he'd woken up, life had made sense. And, yeah, maybe it had been a little messy, but it made sense. Mostly. Now, standing here in the middle of downtown Marietta, with a faint excitement stirring in his gut, he had no clue where to go from here.

He knew he needed to clear his head, maybe go for a ride. And then he wanted to see Rachel. Because if anyone would understand that excitement, it'd be her.

"I'll think about it, cousin," he said. "You've got my word."

Chapter Twelve

"OH MY *GOD*," Chloe sighed and clutched her chest, which was barely contained underneath a sequined Christmas sweater with a plunging neckline. "Get a load of that baby!"

Balancing her tray of drinks, Rachel smiled and looked over her friend's shoulder at the line of expectant families waiting to take their pictures with Santa. The Graff lobby was full of kids—crying kids, happy kids, excited kids, exhausted kids. You name it. If you lived in Marietta, and were under ten, chances were you were dressed in your Sunday best, waiting to tell the big guy what you wanted for Christmas.

It was Saturday night and the weekend of the Marietta Stroll. Outside the hotel, the entire town buzzed with food vendors, people shopping and drinking warm beverages, making their way from the lighting ceremony, which had just taken place in Crawford Park.

Inside the bar, there was a steady stream of folks coming in to get toasty and grab a bite. It was a cold night, but clear as a bell underneath a sky crowded with twinkling stars. The perfect evening for something like this, and the Graff was packed.

"She's so cute," Rachel said, watching the little girl squirm in her dad's arms. She couldn't have been more than a year old, but she had a thick head of blond curls and chubby little legs that were decked out in a pair of bright red tights.

"Doesn't that make you want one?" Chloe sounded wistful.

"A baby?"

"No, a super hot husband, who takes the kids to see Santa."

Rachel laughed. Chloe was nothing if not consistent. But she had to admit, her friend had a point. Something about the young dad and his baby tugged on her heartstrings, too. And made her ovaries ache. She'd always known she wanted to be a mother. But the traditional family part was harder to let herself dream about. In her world, husbands didn't always stick around.

She loved her own father. But, since her parents' divorce, she hadn't seen him much. He'd settled in Florida after retiring from the Army and had met someone else. Started another family. She understood the reality—people changed, relationships died. But she'd always feel protective of her mom, who got the raw end of that deal.

Rachel gazed at the man, who juggled the baby in one arm and a diaper bag in the other. "I wouldn't kick him out of bed for eating crackers," she said.

"Amen, sister."

Across the lobby, Bob waved at them. He was wearing

one of his signature light-up ties and a green blazer.

Chloe and Rachel wiggled their fingers back.

"He's in his element," Chloe said. "He looks like a human Christmas tree."

"But he can pull it off."

"That's true. I'm having a hard enough time in this sweater."

"Oh, come on. You know you look gorgeous."

Chloe smiled and primly touched her hair. She smelled like a sugar cookie. "Well, I try. I'm not a brilliant podcaster. I've got to do what I can with what I've got."

"You think I'm brilliant?"

"I think you're exceptionally brilliant. That episode on the Elliotts; it made me cry. And I never cry."

Rachel grinned. "That's good. Crying is good."

"Very good. And *everyone* is listening to it, Rach. You've got something special on your hands, you know."

It was true that she'd gotten several good reviews in the last few days. And a couple more sponsors in the bag. Her podcast was actually bringing in some money now. Enough for her to invest in a nicer mic and to start putting some money into savings—something she'd never managed before. Who knew what the future would bring? But she was proud of herself for doing this. For striking out on her own, for being self-taught. But, most of all, for risking failure, but tackling it anyway. No matter what happened in the long run, she knew she'd done what she'd set out to, and that was a very good feeling indeed.

"Thanks, Chloe. That means so much."

"It's the truth."

"I've got to get these to table six," she said, "or they'll start throwing a fit. Talk later?"

"Sure thing, babe. Oh, and by the way…I think you've got an admirer at the bar."

Rachel followed her friend's gaze. There, sitting on a barstool between a couple of cowboys, was Lucky. Her belly tightened. He had a big hand wrapped around a beer, and the other splayed across his thigh. And he was looking directly at her. Through all the people in the bar, through all the women who were dressed to their winter nines, that smoldering gaze was for her and her alone.

"Hot damn," Chloe said, shaking her head. "That's one sexy man, Rachel. If you don't do something about that, I might have to."

Rachel's cheeks heated, but she couldn't stop looking at him. "Don't you like his cousin?"

"That's right. I do like his cousin. Those boys have good genes."

"Chloe!" Shane shouted over the Christmas music blasting on the jukebox. She leaned across the bar looking uncharacteristically frazzled. "Help me out with a few beers, will ya?"

"Be right there!" Chloe winked at Rachel and walked away, hips swaying.

Rachel balanced the tray of drinks and held up a finger to Lucky. "One sec?" she mouthed.

He nodded.

Satisfied he wasn't going to leave right away, she made

her way through the crowded bar to a booth where two couples sat waiting. She chatted for a minute, asking if they were having fun at the Stroll, then told them their food would be right up.

With butterflies in her stomach, she turned and headed back to where Lucky sat at the bar.

The place was noisy tonight—louder than usual—and when she stepped up to his barstool, she had to lean in so he could hear. She didn't mind. He smelled like leather and aftershave.

"What are you doing here?" she asked.

"I came to see you."

The simple words warmed her to the core. He'd come to see her. She could get used to him coming to see her.

She pulled away enough to look him in the face. The strong jaw covered in rust-colored stubble. The bright blue eyes. The wide, expressive mouth. She grinned.

He reached up and ran the backs of his knuckles along her cheekbone. He'd barely touched her, but her heart began hammering inside her chest anyway.

"What?" he asked.

"I just thought you might be here because of the Stroll. Does Sleigh Bell have rides tonight?"

"We do, but Pete's taking care of those."

"How's your grandpa?"

"Better. Grandma's got him resting. Doctor's orders. And he's basking in his newfound celebrity from the podcast. Even if he didn't have a huge bump on his head, it'd still be the size of Rhode Island."

She laughed. "We've created a monster?"

"We've created something."

Someone squeezed past. She had to step between Lucky's legs in order to make room. Before she could step back again, he wrapped an arm around her waist and pulled her closer.

"I've missed you," he said into her ear.

Her knees trembled. She could feel his breath against her neck, his thumb making gentle half arcs on her lower back. She was grateful he was holding her upright.

"Oh, yeah?" she managed.

"Yeah. And I have something I want to tell you."

"What?"

"Not here," he said. "Will you go to dinner with me? In the next few days, whenever you're free."

"I'm off Wednesday. Would that work?"

"Perfect. Rocco's?"

She loved Rocco's. But she loved the idea of eating there with Lucky more. "Sure."

He smiled. "It's a date."

A date. An official date. She'd need a new dress. And a blowout. And Chloe's never-ending words of wisdom. Dates never phased Chloe. Probably because she had so many of them. Rachel, on the other hand…

She smiled back. "It's a date."

LUCKY RAN A gloved hand over the horse's withers and across his sloping back. Dreamer stood quietly, eating from the hay rack in his stall, and acting like a generally happy soul. In the few weeks since he'd come to Sleigh Bell, the little gelding had improved by leaps and bounds. He'd gained some weight, and his black coat was beginning to fill in and shine with a soft, winter luster. But, most importantly, he was starting to trust people again. For an animal that had been so close to the brink of starvation, who had absolutely no reason to have faith in anyone again, he was finding it, and then some.

Lucky patted the horse's neck. His temperament was special. Very special and, without thinking, Lucky glanced over at the harnesses hanging in the tack room. Dreamer liked Pop Tart. They'd bonded quickly since he'd been here, and Lucky kept coming back to the idea of training him to pull a sleigh. With Pop Tart teaching him the ropes, he might be a natural.

But every time he went there, he had to yank himself back again. Nothing was set in stone yet—not the sanctuary, not Dreamer's future. And sure as hell not Lucky's future. He just needed to take a few days to come to peace with where his heart wanted to go. And where his brain said he should go. He thought he knew. But he needed to make absolutely sure.

"I thought you might be out here."

Dreamer looked up, a piece of hay sticking out of his mouth, and pricked his ears toward the barn door.

Lucky waved his grandmother over, scraping some dirt from the horse's shoulder with a curry comb. "Over here. Just having a spa day."

His grandma smiled and walked up holding a carrot. Dreamer craned his neck over the stall door and gobbled it up, then immediately sniffed for more.

"That's it, or you're gonna get fat," she said. But scratched his whiskery chin in a way that said she didn't much care if he did get fat, and would be back with more carrots to prove it.

"He likes you," Lucky said.

"He likes carrots."

"He likes you *and* carrots."

She wrapped her southwestern-print sweater around her, before pulling up a stool and sitting with a sigh.

"I just got off the phone with Jake," she said. "He's worried about us."

"I think he's got good reason to be, Grandma."

"I know. What happened the other night was a wakeup call."

Lucky ran the brush over the horse's mane and watched the dust rise into the air like smoke. "I'm just glad it wasn't worse."

"Me too."

A peaceful silence settled over them for a minute. The farm was quiet under the new blanket of snow outside, and the barn felt cozy with the warmth of the animals inside. Dave and Betsy were a few stalls down, munching on some grain and enjoying their new retirement. Stitch was curled up in a bed of hay next to the tack room, chasing something in his dreams. At that moment, Lucky couldn't imagine anything else but running this place until the day he died.

He almost opened his mouth to say it. Almost. But stopped when his grandma spoke first.

"The podcast was just lovely," she said. "It sure doesn't feel like we've been married sixty-five years. In a lot of ways, I still feel like a girl."

"You still look like a girl, Grandma."

She grinned and waved him away. "Oh, you."

Laughing, he tossed the brush back in the bucket and gave Dreamer a pat.

"I never thought when we inherited this place, we'd be here for the long haul," she continued. "Farm life hasn't always been easy. But it's been good to us. Raising our kids and grandkids on Sleigh Bell was the best thing we ever did." She paused, as if looking for the right words. As if she wanted to be careful with them. "But we're going to have to talk about this place, you know. It's something we've been putting off, because nobody wants to admit what's coming. But it's coming just the same."

He settled his gaze on hers and felt his mouth settle into a hard line.

"I know your dad has put pressure on you, Lucky," she said, her voice low.

He swallowed and looked down at his boots for a few seconds before looking back up. "He wants what's best for us. I understand that."

"Yes. He does. But he's always held you to a different standard than the rest of the boys, and that hasn't been fair to you all these years."

He smiled, trying to lighten the moment. "I'm just a

wild card. You know."

She didn't smile with him. "But you're not. You never were."

"I've made mistakes."

"We've all made mistakes, son."

No matter how many years went by, no matter how much daylight opened up between the day of the fire and today, Lucky could never seem to outrun the careless boy he'd been. No matter how much he tried to prove to himself that he'd grown. No matter how much he tried to prove to his family that he'd changed. And his grandmother could see it. She always could.

He wondered honestly then, what it was going to take for him to truly heal. To move on, like Patrick had said. Becoming a successful vet? Or dreaming, and risking everything he'd worked his whole life for?

He eyed his grandmother. "Why are you saying this now?"

"Because Jake is coming home next week. All the boys will be home for Christmas soon. Your parents. Everyone. We'll be getting together as a family. Maybe it's time you decide what it is you really want, Lucky."

He hadn't mentioned the sanctuary. But it was beginning to look like he didn't need to. Maybe it was written all over his damn face.

Nodding, he turned to the little mustang, who was defying odds as they spoke. There was absolutely no reason why Dreamer couldn't be trained to pull a sleigh. No reason why he couldn't do that, even though it'd be hard. Even though it'd test him some. So why was Lucky so hell bent on taking the safest route with his own life? He knew the answer to that. But it didn't make it any easier to accept.

He clenched his jaw so hard it hurt. If he wasn't careful, he'd be eighty before he knew it. And unlike his grandmother, he'd have a lifetime of regrets to show for it.

Chapter Thirteen

LUCKY PULLED UP to the small apartment complex on Railway Avenue with a couple of minutes to spare. It wasn't quite seven yet, and he was glad. He found himself wanting to savor the moment. He was picking up a beautiful woman for a first date. Someone he wanted to get to know better. Wanted to kiss again. And she seemed like she might want the same. It was something he didn't want to rush.

The sun had set behind Copper Mountain a few hours ago, leaving the sky a velvety black. The stars were out, scattered across the heavens like rhinestones. It was like a cosmic dress that Mother Earth had slipped on for just this occasion.

The air was biting cold, and when he opened his truck door, it nearly stole the breath from his lungs. But Rachel had been adamant about walking to Rocco's tonight. The sidewalks were clear and salted, and the Christmas lights glowed softly through town from every direction. He hadn't argued.

Locking his truck, he headed up her walkway. The apartments were cute—bungalow style, surrounded by towering blue spruces and Ponderosa pines. In the dark like this, with the mountains nothing but shadows in the distance, Lucky could almost see what Marietta must've looked like a hundred years ago. Back when the Graff was the most elegant place in town and the Sleigh Bell land was wild and rugged. He wondered if his great, great grandparents had any idea, when they'd settled here in their cabin on the hill, that they were setting in motion a family saga that would still be playing out over a century later. Lucky was proud of their farm. And tonight, standing on Rachel's doorstep getting ready to knock, he felt like he might be on the verge of something special.

He took a breath, but before he could raise his fist to knock, the door opened in a flood of yellow light and perfumed air.

Rachel stood there, in a floral dress and cowboy boots. Her hair was pulled up in a messy bun, and small gold hoops flashed in her earlobes. Her lips were darker tonight than usual. A deep berry color that made him want to kiss her. She was so damn beautiful, he could only stare for a minute, wondering how in the world he'd gotten so lucky.

"I was watching from the window," she said, grinning. "I'm kind of excited. Want to come in for a minute? I need to grab my jacket."

He stepped inside her entryway, unable to take his eyes off her.

She touched her hair self-consciously. "Too much?"

"No," he said, his mouth dry. "Just right."

She reached for a thick, suede jacket on the end table and slipped it on. Then wrapped a pink scarf around her neck.

She looked like a Christmas present.

He glanced around her apartment, which was small, but cozy. The couch had colorful throw pillows tossed in the corners. The curtains were bright and cheerful, and the pictures hanging on the walls were watercolors of various places in Marietta. He recognized them immediately—the fairgrounds where the rodeo took place, Bramble House Bed and Breakfast, Miracle Lake in the winter, and of course, the Graff. And there was a Christmas tree in the window, its white lights twinkling.

He felt something rub against his ankles, and he looked down to see a calico cat looking back up. She meowed expectantly.

"Well, hi there." He bent down to give her a scratch. "What's your name?"

"That's Lucy," Rachel said.

"Ahh. *The* Lucille Ball, huh? The queen of comedy."

Rachel laughed. "I don't know about comedy, but queen of her domain, for sure."

"As it should be." The little cat rammed her head into Lucky's palm, and he rubbed her ears for another second before straightening to see Rachel watching him.

"What?"

"Nothing," she said. "It's just...I don't know. Sexy, I guess. The way you are with animals."

He smiled and stepped forward, closing the gap between them. Looking down at her, he touched the tip of her nose.

"Sexy, huh? I could probably use that to my advantage."

Her cheeks colored, her freckles almost disappearing in

front of his eyes. "I wouldn't complain."

He slipped an arm around her waist and leaned toward her mouth. She smelled like vanilla. Like warmth and summertime. Her lips were full and glistening under the soft light of the room. Her eyes were dark and expectant. He had to fight the sudden urge to unwrap her scarf so he could kiss the delicate hollow of her throat.

"You're pretty sexy too," he said.

She watched him, waiting. He thought she might be shaking some, and he pulled her closer. God, she was gorgeous. He knew if he gave in to this, whatever it was, things wouldn't be the same moving forward. He welcomed that. But he also feared it. Because messing around with a woman like Rachel would complicate things. Plenty.

Still, he bent the rest of the way and kissed her like he'd wanted to since walking through the door.

With a small sigh, she relaxed in his arms and parted her lips. She was soft and giving. Painfully feminine. But he also felt a quiet strength in her that was significant. Rachel could hold her own. And she wasn't afraid to go after what she wanted. He liked that.

She reached up and touched his face, ran her fingertips along his jawline. Made him feel like taking off his coat, and hers too. He wanted to explore that quiet strength, feel it underneath his hands.

Slowly, painfully, he broke the kiss and pulled away. He was afraid, if he didn't, they might end up on the couch, or even better, the bedroom. And he really wanted to take her to dinner. To buy her a glass of wine and tell her all the things that had been churning in his brain since he'd stood outside the fire station a few days ago.

She smiled. And it lit up her entire face. "I'm starving," she said.

"Me too."

She really had no idea.

THEY WALKED SIDE by side up Main Street, headed toward Rocco's, where Rachel was pretty sure she could smell the calzone baking from inside the kitchen. Or maybe that was just wishful thinking, since they were still more than a block away.

She'd been honest before. She *was* starving. But all she really cared about now was the sound of Lucky's low laughter beside her and the way he kept looking over. Like he was genuinely happy to be out with her tonight. Like she might disappear if he took his gaze off her long enough. It made her feel special, coveted. And she really, really loved that.

She'd known before, of course. The fact that she'd end up falling for him. Because really, you couldn't *not* fall for Lucky. She felt like she was on a bobsled barreling down a mountain at ninety miles an hour. One wrong move, and she'd tumble out of control. Nothing to do now except hope and pray that she'd have some common sense where he was concerned. Some way to put the brakes on if she needed to.

He walked so close, that his arm kept brushing hers. The night was cold, but lovely. In true Marietta fashion, there were people out enjoying it. Sipping hot chocolates and taking advantage of the holiday store hours. Across the street, the Sleigh Bell carriage sat waiting for new passengers. Tonight, two horses decked out in festive harnesses were hitched to it.

She watched them, dipping her chin into her scarf for extra warmth. "Aww. No more Dave and Betsy, huh?"

He smiled. "Nope. They're living the life. This is a temporary team—they don't have the best temperament for harness work, but we'll get it sorted out. We miss the donkeys, though."

"It's nice they're retiring in such a peaceful place. So many animals don't have that…"

She hadn't meant it to be a suggestive comment about the sanctuary. But once the words were out, they both looked at each other.

Lucky's breath puffed from his mouth in a silver cloud. "It is a peaceful place, isn't it?"

His normally long strides shortened beside hers. And then he stopped and looked up at the starry sky above. She looked up, too, and, for a second, she was lost in the sparkling galaxy overhead. Where anything was possible. Where dreams came true if you wished hard enough for them. Or worked hard enough for them.

"I've been thinking a lot these last few days," he said. "Actually, I've been thinking a lot these last few years, but it wasn't until I met you that I started chewing on things that I'd been afraid of before."

At the tone of his voice, she looked over. Cars passed,

blowing cold swooshes of air against her legs. Shivering, she pulled her jacket tighter.

"What do you mean?"

Slowly, he took his gaze from the sky, and settled it on her.

"I mean, I've been thinking more about the sanctuary."

She was almost afraid to believe that. "You have?"

"I have." He put his hands in his pockets and exhaled a slow breath. "I went to see Patrick the other day. He said he'd go in on it with me. That he'd help run it. I don't know…with him as a partner, it just might work."

She felt herself smiling like an idiot.

He smiled back. "Nothing's set in stone yet. I still have to talk to my family. There's a lot of us, and if anyone had a problem with it, it'd have to stop right there. Before it even got started."

"I know. But this is a really big step."

He reached for her hand and pulled her close. He smelled faintly of aftershave, and his body was warm and solid.

"If I hadn't met you, Rachel," he continued, "none of this would be happening. I wouldn't even have the courage to mull it over. I still need to do what's best for the farm, and I have to be open to the fact this might not be it. But at least I'm going to pitch it to my family, which is a lot more than I would've done otherwise. Without you, I would've gone back to school and lived the rest of my life wondering what if. Now, I won't have to. Now I'll know."

She stood on her tiptoes and put her arms around his

neck. "I'm so, so proud of you, Lucky."

The look in his eyes warmed instantly. At her touch, at her words, she didn't know which. But he leaned down the rest of the way and kissed her so tenderly, that her heart ached because of it.

After a few seconds, he pulled away and pushed her hair back from her temple. His expression was naked and vulnerable.

"You're so damn beautiful," he said.

Nobody, in her whole entire life, had made her feel as sexy as he'd made her feel right then. It was like she was waking up after a long, cold sleep. Realizing things about herself that she'd never known before. With him, she felt like she could take flight at any moment. And watch the world from below her outstretched wings.

"You have to stop saying things like that," she said, looking at his mouth. "Or…"

He brushed her lips with his. Once, twice, then leaned away, breaking her heart at the distance of only a few inches. "Or, what?"

She laughed, shaking her head and looking away. "You know. You've always known."

"I want you to say it."

His voice was serious. So serious that her belly tightened at the sound. He did want her to say it. He wanted her to say it, and he wanted to see her saying it. Somehow, the moment was incredibly erotic, sensual. Add that to the list of things she'd never been before. Erotic.

She swallowed the cotton ball in her throat and forced

herself to look him in the eyes. By that simple act, she felt the balance of power between them shift so subtly, that it felt like moth wings brushing against her heart. "Or I'm going to end up falling in love with you."

He watched her. A couple walked by, their bags rustling in the night air. From somewhere down the street a dog barked, followed by distant laughter. The town was alive around them, moving and breathing. But, at that second, it was just the two of them. Watching each other. Absorbing the moment. What it meant. Or what it could mean if they were to let it have its way.

"I've never been in love before," he said.

She wasn't going to let that scare her off. Not now. Not after that kiss. She was going to match him stride for stride. "I have. I fall in love a lot, actually."

His lips twitched and he nodded slowly.

"I think it's because I'm always looking for it," she continued, "whether I want to find it or not. But I've never found *true* love. And there's a difference."

"And what does true love look like?"

"Like how your grandparents look at each other. Like how my friend Bob looks at a Christmas tree."

He laughed at that.

"Or what Dave and Betsy have. It's something that doesn't come along every day, but that lasts, even when a relationship ends. I've seen it so many times doing my podcast. So many times, that it's impossible not to believe in it anymore. Even if it hasn't happened to me, I know it's out there."

He smoothed one of her eyebrows with his thumb. "You know something?"

"What?"

"I think you're pretty amazing."

And there it was. The moment when falling for him became tumbling. Down, down, toward something that beckoned like a long-lost friend. Good or bad, this was where she was meant to be. Right here, right now. Feeling exactly like this.

She grazed her teeth over her bottom lip trying to look like that hadn't just jarred her right out of her boots. But he could probably tell anyway.

"I think you're amazing, too," she said.

He grinned, that devilish, panty-dropping grin of his. "So, we're both amazing. Now what?"

She took his hand. "Now we go to dinner. We have a glass of wine. And we toast to the possibility of you running an animal sanctuary on your farm. We toast Patrick, we toast the podcast. We toast your grandparents…"

"And we toast you. For bringing us to this point."

They stared at each other for another few seconds. A car went by, kicking up some slush, but Lucky pulled her away before it spattered on her dress.

"That was close."

Rachel nodded, suddenly cold. "I should've worn galoshes. It's so wet tonight."

"Tomorrow it'll all be ice. Come on. Let's get that wine." He put his arm around her and they began walking toward Rocco's underneath the sliver of a winter moon.

They started talking about his family, how they'd be home for Christmas soon. They talked about the farm, and how growing up on Sleigh Bell, in Marietta, had shaped who he was, who he wanted to be. He held her close while they walked, keeping her warm, making her feel safe. It was like they'd always been like this. On the verge of something more. She felt the stirring of it in her heart.

They slowed at the corner of Main and First, waiting for the light to change. The entrance to Grey's was only a few feet away, and the music thumped out the swinging doors into the cold night air. There was a live band tonight, and they were playing something Christmassy, with a country flare.

Behind them, a car revved its engine. Rachel looked over. Probably a teenager doing their best to push boundaries.

The light changed, and she stepped off the curb. But, when the motor gunned again, Lucky pulled her back.

The car sped past in a squeal of tires on wet cement, and before Rachel could process what was happening, they were soaked in dirty puddle water.

"Aww, shit," Lucky said, holding his arms out. He was drenched.

She stared down at her dress. It clung to her legs. There was freezing water standing in her boots. She wiggled her toes, and they squished in her socks.

She gaped at Lucky.

"Shit," he repeated. "I'd give you my coat, but…"

Shivering, she laughed. They probably looked so ridiculous standing there like two drowned rats. It was the only thing *to* do.

"Okay," he said. "Change of plans. But first, change of clothes."

She hugged herself.

"Your place or mine?"

Chapter Fourteen

RACHEL WIPED AWAY the condensation from her bathroom mirror and stared at her reflection with a frown. This wasn't how tonight was supposed to have gone. She and Lucky were supposed to be having a drink right now under the romantic lighting in Rocco's. Toasting to the sanctuary and all the joy and excitement that went along with it.

Instead, her mascara was smudged under her eyes, and her hair lay in dripping tendrils against the back of her neck. And her dress, which lay in a sad little pile in the corner, was probably ruined. But at least she'd been able to have a shower, so they could try and salvage their date.

Lucy, who always insisted on coming into the bathroom with her, sat and licked a dainty paw. From down the hall, Rachel could hear the dryer whirring. Lucky had put his shirt in there. Which meant he wasn't wearing one at the moment.

At the thought, her mouth went dry, and she fought against the fluttering of her pulse. It was still better to try and slow down where Lucky was concerned. Even if all she really wanted was to let him remove her underwear with his teeth.

Raising her chin, she forced her shoulders back. "Lucy, we're strong women, right?"

The cat blinked up at her, then gave a small mew in agreement.

"Absolutely we are. We can compartmentalize this situation. Easy peasy."

She looked back in the mirror. Tiny droplets of water clung to her pale skin, and her eyes, framed with wet, spiked lashes, seemed darker than usual. She told herself that didn't have anything to do with the fact that she was naked, with Lucky in the next room. But even she had to admit, it was hard to explain away. Lucky was in the next room. *Fact.* And she was naked. *Fact.* Inconvenient, yes. But true.

Staring at herself, she narrowed her eyes. This was ridiculous. She'd get dressed like a normal person and go out to offer him a cup of coffee while they waited for his shirt to dry. Then they'd head to Rocco's. No biggie. She just had to go out there and pretend all these things hadn't crossed her mind just now. And that her heart wasn't beating out a traitorous rhythm inside her chest.

Bending down, she reached for her change of clothes. But then her heart stopped beating all together. *Crap, crap, crap!*

Standing up straight, she stared at her reflection again. And this time, her eyes were wide as saucers. She'd forgotten to bring her change of clothes into the bathroom with her. She'd been too distracted by the ever-present image of Lucky taking off his shirt. Which meant she had *nothing* to change into. Nothing, that is, except her muddy, sopping dress, or the towel she'd dried off with.

Impervious, Lucy began weaving in between her ankles. Rachel planted her hands on either side of the sink. It wasn't funny. But it kind of was.

She took a deep breath. Okay. She had a few choices, here. One, she could ask Lucky to get some clothes for her. Which wasn't exactly tempting, since she'd also have to ask him to dig through her underwear drawer. Two, she could wrap herself in the towel and walk past him to get her clothes herself. Optimal? No. But doable. Surely he'd seen his fair share of women in towels before. Which, didn't make her feel any better, but still.

Or three... She settled her gaze on the red terrycloth robe hanging on the back of the door. It had been an early Christmas present from Chloe. And she hadn't counted it as something to wear before because it barely covered her butt. It was that short. *And* the hood had antler horns on it. Antler horns. So. There was that.

She stared at it. Unfortunately, it was looking like her best bet right now. Unless her cat suddenly sprouted opposing thumbs and went to fetch some undies for her, this was it.

Miserably, she reached for the robe and slipped it on. Then secured the tie snugly around her waist.

She finger-combed her wet hair and rubbed the mascara smudges away from her eyes. At least she was clean. At least there was that. She'd been a hot mess before she'd stepped in the shower. Lucky, on the other hand, had looked complete-ly edible with his small, dark nipples showing through the wet spots in his white western shirt, that had been crisp as a new bill when he'd picked her up earlier.

She took a steadying breath, then scolded herself for it. She was overthinking this. She really was. She'd just grab her clothes and get dressed.

Opening the door, she peeked down the hallway toward the living room. Her little Christmas tree glowed in front of the window, its lights sparkling like precious stones. Music was coming from the stereo, something soft and festive. She'd forgotten that she'd left it on earlier to keep Lucy company.

The cat bolted past her. Apparently, she shared none of her mistress's apprehension. In fact, she seemed drawn to Lucky, like everyone else.

Rachel swallowed and walked toward the music, her bare feet padding on the hardwood floor.

She came around the corner to see him standing at the darkened window, gazing out. His back was to her, and he had his thumbs hooked in the pockets of his dark washed Wranglers. His skin was pale, with a spattering of freckles across his broad, muscular shoulders.

Her heart tapped in the hollow of her throat. He was beautiful, like she'd known he would be. Muscled and hard. His waist narrow and tapering where the jeans sat low on his hips. And it was there that her gaze caught as if on a jagged piece of glass. Scar tissue, pink and puckered, snaked around his middle.

For one awful minute, she tried to remember if she'd insisted that he take his shirt off and use her dryer. Had she made him feel uncomfortable somehow? Maybe he'd wanted to go back to Sleigh Bell to change instead?

She opened her mouth to say something, but stopped when her eyes met his in the reflection of the window. He was looking right at her. And his expression wasn't one of embarrassment or hesitation. It was one of extreme male confidence. And desire. She could see it in the set of his mouth, the slight tilt of his head. In the way he didn't turn around, but held her gaze like a rabbit in a snare. She was trapped by him. And she didn't want to fight it.

"I…" She couldn't remember what she'd been about to say. It didn't matter anyway. Because he turned then, slowly, like he'd been waiting for this moment. Maybe they both had.

The scars across his chest were considerable. They looked hot, tender to the touch, stretching over his extensive muscle and bone like an intruder. And all she could think of was him trapped in that fire as a boy. Almost dying. Unable to come to terms with the financial toll it had taken on his family, for the trauma he'd put them through. And for the animals that were lost. She wanted to pull that boy into her arms, to hug him close, and tell him that it was okay. It was all going to be okay.

But that Lucky was long gone. The man standing before her now was unapologetic for the painful map of memories that lay across his body. In fact, he clenched his jaw as he watched her, maybe looking for signs that she wasn't ready for this. For him, in all his complexity and layers.

His fevered gaze slid down her body and back up again.

She was aware of her chest rising and falling where the robe gaped open. Where her breasts swelled against the terrycloth fabric. Her nipples pebbled against her will, and she knew he'd be able to see their sharp points clearly enough from where he stood.

Her gaze dropped to his stomach where a dark line of hair ran down his muscled abdomen. An arrow, pointing down, down, to where his jeans hid the rest of him from view.

God. She could barely believe this was happening. They'd just come back here to dry off, that was all. But, at the same time, she knew something had been set in motion between them from the moment they'd met. Sparks that were going to catch fire, whether they liked it or not.

Lucky's lips tilted. Just a little, but the sexiness of that smile was about all she could take.

"Can I just say, thank Jesus for trucks without mud flaps," he said, his voice smooth as scotch.

"I was just...I was just going to grab my clothes from the bedroom."

He looked at the hood of her robe. "Are those..."

"Antlers," she said. "Reindeer antlers."

"Of course they are."

"I don't normally wear reindeer antlers. Just so you know."

His eyes twinkled, shadows from the Christmas tree lights playing across his face. "I don't give a damn about the antlers, Rachel. I'm more interested in those legs."

She shifted on her feet, feeling like she needed to move

underneath his gaze. Like she'd need to move underneath his body if he were on top of her right that minute. *Lord, have mercy.* How she wanted that. She no longer cared if he could read it in her eyes. Or in the flush of her skin. Or the rise and fall of her breasts. She wanted him. Everything he was willing to give.

He held out his hand. "Come here."

She hesitated, because her brain was still arguing with her heart… *Be careful…you know better…*

But it only took a second for her libido to win out. She stepped forward, trying to remember to breathe, but it wasn't easy. She felt light-headed, dizzy.

She put her hand in his. She didn't think she'd ever get used to the feeling of standing this close, and how it made her want to kiss the darkest, sweetest parts of his body.

He pulled her against him, wrapping an arm around her lower back. She didn't look up right away. She was having trouble taking her gaze from his chest, from the beauty of it. And the pain.

She must've frowned, because he put a finger under her chin and tilted it upward.

"I know it's hard to look at" he said, his voice husky. "Just don't. Look up here."

"It's not hard to look at. You're not hard to look at."

He brushed her hair away from her face. "It is what it is. You get used to it."

"I think you're perfect." It was more than she'd meant to say, but the truth always found its way to the surface. *Always.*

"That's where you're wrong, baby. I'm not."

Baby... A slow heat built in her chest, as he traced her jawline with the tips of his fingers.

He leaned close. His minty breath was warm against her face, and she found she wanted to beg for something, but she didn't even know what she wanted. Only that she needed it, needed him, more than he could ever know.

"Hey," he said. "Look at me."

She'd been staring at his mouth. But when he spoke, she slid her gaze up to meet his.

"You don't have to be worried about this. We can take it slow. We can change into our dry clothes and go to dinner just like we'd planned." He smiled then. "It won't be easy, but I'll make myself forget seeing you like this. If that's what you want."

Her face burned. But it felt like stepping close to a fire after being out in the cold for days. She welcomed every pinprick tingle on her skin, every deep flush. This was what he did to her.

Was getting dressed and going to dinner and sticking to her very safe, very practical plan, what she wanted? She wasn't so sure anymore. She was terrified of falling any harder for Lucky than she already had. But, for some reason, this didn't feel as dangerous as it might have a few weeks ago. After all, he was officially thinking about the sanctuary. That didn't mean he'd actually go through with it. But it proved he might be on the same page as her. That he was at least considering building a life in Marietta, a town she knew they both loved. And that he was thinking of reaching for the brightest star—a dream not everyone thought was practical.

She identified with that on the most profound level.

So, she swallowed down the response that would've been automatic with anyone else. *Yes, let's not rush it. Let's go to dinner, okay?* Instead, with her heart slamming in her chest, she brought his hand up to her breast where the robe gaped open.

His pupils exploded, swallowing his irises whole. And he squeezed her gently.

"I don't want to be anywhere else right now," she said. "I just want to be with you."

At that, he finally kissed her, his tongue flicking against her lips. Then, in one fluid motion, he picked her up. Literally, swept her off her feet, and cradled her against his chest.

She wrapped both arms around his neck and put her hands in his hair—red enough to come by the Irish nickname honestly. The Christmas music on the stereo switched to something softer, making her think of a warmly lit cabin in the snow.

"Are you sure, Rachel?" he murmured against her throat.

Shivering, she closed her eyes. He was doing everything right. Everything. She'd only ever experienced something like this in her dreams—in those subconscious moments where fantasy reigned supreme and she woke up barely able to catch her breath.

"Yes," she said. "I'm sure."

Chapter Fifteen

T HREE LITTLE WORDS. But they were so significant.

Lucky stared down at her. She was so beautiful, so delicate-looking in the dim light of the room. But she wasn't delicate. Not by a long shot. She was a woman who knew what she wanted and worked her rear end off to get it. She was smart, talented, driven. The real deal. And if anyone could make him want things he wasn't exactly comfortable with yet, it was her.

He bounced her against his chest, making her laugh, and stepped over to the couch where he lay her down. He loved how dark her eyes looked as she took him in. She didn't seem to mind the scars.

He leaned over her to close the curtains, and she reached up to touch his stomach. He pulled in a breath as she traced the line of hair above his belt with her fingertips.

Clenching his jaw, he looked down at her. Her hair was still wet, and she wore no makeup. He could smell her shampoo, something fruity and sweet, that made him want to bury his face in her neck. He wanted to feel the silkiness of her skin against his. But most of all, he wanted to hear her say his name.

Slowly, he lowered himself down, and she wrapped her legs around the backs of his thighs. His belt had to be digging into her belly, but she clung to him so tightly that all he could do was lie there and kiss her.

Small sounds escaped her throat as he shifted and moved the robe aside, once and for all. He cupped her breast, which was plump and warm, her nipple hardening immediately against his palm.

She ran her hands down his back, touching the scar tissue at his hip softly, tenderly. Then reached down and unbuckled his belt. Pulling it through the loops with a soft *shwoop,* she dropped it on the floor. At the sound, the cat bolted into the kitchen.

Rachel laughed. "I don't think she's used to this kind of excitement on a Saturday night."

He smiled against her lips. Then slid a hand down her ribcage, making her arch into him with a gasp. He reached lower, lower, until he felt the soft curve of her hipbone underneath his fingers.

Nuzzling behind her ear, he breathed her in. *Sweet Rachel.* So lovely, so full of life. What if he wasn't good enough for her? No matter what he ended up doing with the sanctuary, or the farm, or vet school, maybe he'd never be good enough. He knew what she thought of him, and he was afraid of disappointing her. Of disappointing his parents and grandparents. He wanted to be the man they all deserved.

"Lucky..." she whispered.

It wasn't the name he wanted to hear. But he didn't think he'd ever be able to say that to her. Or anyone, for that matter. Inside, he longed to be seen, to be known for who he really was. But she was as close as anyone had ever gotten until now. Even his own grandfather, who'd always been able to read him like an open book, didn't have the insight Rachel did.

"What?" he asked.

"Please…"

He knew what she wanted, because he wanted it too. Without another word, he pushed his hand lower. She arched underneath him. Her legs opened wider, her knees trembling on either side of him.

"Lucky," she said again.

He wished he could keep her safe in his arms like this for as long as she'd stay. But would he stay himself? For the long haul? Or was that too much of a commitment for a man who got by on dry humor and keeping people at an arm's length? He didn't know. He only knew how he felt in this moment. Like the world had been turned on its ear.

She lifted her head off the couch to kiss his neck, his jaw. And then he shifted, trying to keep as much of his weight off her as possible, as he moved over her.

Everything about her felt so right. Good, and right, and precious underneath him. It felt like his chest was splitting open, like his whole body was opening to her. He kissed her eyebrow, her cheek, the tip of her nose. And then he found her mouth again.

And claimed it for his own.

"DID YOU HEAR what I just said?"

Rachel looked over at Chloe in a haze. Actually, she'd been in said haze for two days now, going on three. And whenever she caught her reflection in a mirror, or in the frosted windows of the Graff, she'd even say she was glowing.

She just hoped everyone at work couldn't tell. But it was no use. By the way Chloe was watching her now, she might as well have it written across her forehead. *I slept with Lucky Elliott! And, oh. By the way, I think I'm in love with him too.*

"Hmm?"

"I *said*, do you have all your Christmas shopping done? You always wait until the last minute."

"Oh," Rachel said, picking up an empty beer mug and putting on her tray. "Yes. All finished."

Chloe narrowed her eyes.

Uh oh. Here it comes...

"What's going on with you?" her friend asked.

"Nothing."

"Come on. Tell me."

"There's nothing to tell."

"Baloney."

Rachel looked around. It was between the lunch and dinner rush, so the bar was empty. But still.

"Chloe, shhh."

Chloe put her hands on her hips. "Don't you shush me."

"What are we talking about?"

They both turned at the sound of Bob's voice. He sauntered toward them wearing a bright red sweater with a Santa pin on the collar.

Rachel sighed. "Nothing. We're not talking about anything."

Bob sidled up next to Chloe, then began studying Rachel like she was a math problem.

"What?" she asked, her cheeks heating. Was it *that* obvious?

"You look different," Bob said.

"She does," Chloe agreed. "Fundamentally."

"I don't look different!"

"She's been acting weird for the last two days," Chloe said.

Bob nodded, not taking his eyes off her.

"You guys…"

"And she won't tell me what's going on."

"Oh, I already *know,*" Bob said, cocking his head to the side and looking her up and down.

"The podcast?" Chloe asked.

Bob glanced over at her. "Girl, please."

"Both of you *stop,*" Rachel said. "If I tell you, will you drop it? At least until I can get these tables bussed?"

Chloe crossed her arms over her chest, waiting. Her lips were pursed. She looked like a schoolteacher waiting for an explanation. A good one.

Bob, on the other hand, looked like the cat who ate the canary. He couldn't stop smiling, practically bouncing on the toes of his oxfords.

Rachel took a deep breath. She'd never kept any secrets from Chloe. And yeah, it had only been two days. But with them, the record was more like two minutes.

"I slept with Lucky."

"I *knew* it!" Bob whisper-yelled.

"Rach!" Chloe stared at her wide-eyed, incredulous.

"I know, I know. I wanted to tell you. But, at the same time, I was afraid to. If I said anything, it'd make it real. And the more real it is, the better chance I'll get my heart pulverized."

"I can't believe you didn't say anything," Chloe said. "You always tell me your stuff."

"I know I do. I know."

Chloe let this settle. The hurt look on her face quickly shifted to one of acceptance. Then to excitement.

"Thank God," Bob said, clutching his chest. "Thank *God.* I mean, I could tell something was different about this one from the beginning. And all that pent-up sexual frustration isn't good for you. I was about to enroll you in a Zumba class or something."

She laughed. "Well. Thanks for that."

Chloe grabbed her hand. "When do you see him again?"

"His family is coming into town for Christmas, so it'll be a busy week. But soon. I'm supposed to go with him to Mistletoe and Montana. Sleigh Bell has a tree entered this year."

"And he's called?" Chloe asked this hesitantly. And with a slight edge to her voice—like she might have to track him down and kill him if he hadn't.

"He's called. And texted. And sent flowers. He's doing everything right."

"Flowers?" Bob sighed. "Do *not* let this one get away."

Rachel ran a hand through her hair, smoothing it. A nervous habit. Because talking about Lucky getting away, or Lucky *wanting* to get away, scared her. What would she do if this was just a fling for him? How would she ever get over that? Over him?

Bob reached out and patted her arm. "I'm really happy for you, Rach. You deserve this, you know."

She wasn't so sure. Rachel had always had a skewed sense of reality when it came to men and what she did or didn't deserve. She could thank her parents' marriage for that one. At some point she was just going to have to figure it out on her own. She only hoped Lucky wouldn't be the one to teach her any more hard lessons.

"Thanks, Bob," she said. "What would I do without you guys?"

Chapter Sixteen

LUCKY STOOD IN front of the fireplace, planted his hands on the scarred wood mantle, and took a deep breath.

The old house was buzzing. Everyone was home for Christmas. This year the festivities were kicking off early with Mistletoe and Montana at the Graff, and a late dinner afterwards. All three of his brothers were here, as well as several cousins, most of his aunts and uncles, and his parents.

A cacophony of voices spilled from the kitchen, where his grandma had just finished serving eggnog. The house smelled spicy and warm. Everyone was dressed up, and there was a general feeling of happiness inside the walls where he'd felt most at home since childhood.

Clenching his jaw, he listened as the family began making their way into the living room.

"Okay, Luck," his cousin Jenny said, coming up behind him and poking him in the ribs. "What's this all about?"

He'd called a family meeting a few minutes ago. Something they used to do growing up in order to get everyone to listen when something important needed saying. Sometimes it was something as simple as a D in math. But over the years, the meetings had become more serious. This living room was where Jake had announced he was going to rodeo professionally, which had nearly caused their mother to swoon on the floral print couch. It was also where his aunt Jackie told them she'd been diagnosed with Alzheimer's.

But more often than not, it was a happy place to break news. Pregnancies, engagements, job offers had all been announced in this living room, underneath a large painting of a Sleigh Bell carriage that his grandpa had commissioned almost thirty years ago. Lucky hoped today would be another happy occasion. Something to celebrate with the people he loved the most. He'd thought about asking Rachel to come out for just this reason, but hadn't out of hesitation it might not go well. There was always that possibility.

He turned away from the mantle, and saw his sizable family gathered around. Jake was sitting on the couch, his long legs stretched out in front of him. He wore his signature cowboy boots and a starched white shirt with ivory buttons. He'd left his hat at the door, but the tell-tale ring lingered around his strawberry blond hair.

His other brothers, Jesse and Jack, stood next to the coffee table, eggnog in hand. Spiked, no doubt. They smiled at him, looking older, smoother around the edges than Jake. But the family resemblance was undeniable. All four of them looked more like their dad, a tall, wiry redhead, than their mother, who was petite and blonde.

Smiling back, he glanced over at Patrick, who gazed back steadily. His cousin was still on board. Lucky had talked to him again yesterday, and everything was set. He just needed to take the plunge.

Taking a step forward, his chest tightened as his father walked into the room. Broad shouldered, strong features. Piercing blue eyes, behind heavy framed glasses. Hank Elliott was a good man, a kind man, but he was also intimidating as hell. And even though he loved his sons fiercely, outward signs of affection had never come easily. Deep down, Lucky felt like he'd never forgiven his youngest boy. Even today. Even all these years later.

His grandparents were sitting on the loveseat, looking expectant. He knew they'd probably be proud of this idea. It was the rest of his family he was worried about.

He cleared his throat. "Merry Christmas, everyone. Glad you all made it home."

"Merry Christmas," they said in unison.

His Uncle Hal raised his eggnog in a toast.

Lucky's face warmed. He could feel his shoulder muscles straining underneath his sweater. He'd rehearsed this speech about two dozen times, but it didn't matter. It was never going to be perfect anyway.

This was the moment he'd been waiting for. He was going to open his heart, which he'd spent so much effort guarding since he was ten years old.

"I guess there's no other way to say this, except to come right out with it," he said, his voice low. He looked over at his grandparents. "Grandma and Grandpa have decided to step away from daily work on the farm."

They smiled and nodded in agreement.

"It's a lot," he continued, "and I think we'd all like to see them start enjoying retirement. Maybe take some of those trips Grandma's always talking about."

His grandmother sighed. "Tuscany…"

His mom, who was sitting on the other side of her, patted her knee.

Everyone else in the room looked briefly at one another. Really, this part wasn't a surprise. It'd been coming for a while. It was just a matter of someone saying it out loud. What was coming next, though…

Lucky rubbed the back of his neck. "Now, we need to figure out what we're going to do with Sleigh Bell."

His family was silent, waiting for him to go on. Their gazes, all of them, settled squarely on his shoulders. But his father's felt the heaviest. The most significant. All of his hopes for his sons, his pride in them, his stern expectations…it was all a complicated tangle of emotions that Lucky had been trying to free himself from for years. Today was a first step. And he felt like a shaky colt, trying to get his legs underneath him.

"What if I told you I have an idea that would keep the farm going, but in a much more modern direction?"

There were a few low mutterings.

"The sleigh and carriage ride business are the cornerstone of Sleigh Bell," he continued, "but that will only carry us so far into the future. Things are changing—the economy, the tastes of the tourists who come to Marietta—everything is different than it was even five years ago. There will always be people who love the carriage rides. But there are also going to be more and more people objecting to how the animals are treated."

One of Lucky's aunts huffed, and he held up a hand. "Now we know our donkeys and horses are part of our family," he said, "and we don't give them any more work than they can do comfortably. But our customers don't know that. And that's not their fault. They're animal lovers, which is part, or *all,* of why they want to see Marietta in a carriage pulled by a team of donkeys. The point is, we have to lean into this new mindset. It's a good thing to be shining the light on animal welfare, I think we can all agree on that. And Sleigh Bell can thrive and grow, doing just that. Being compassionate advocates of all animals in our care."

His grandmother clutched her chest. She knew what was coming. Maybe she'd always known. In that moment, Lucky felt at peace. Finally. The sanctuary was his calling. It just was. Becoming a vet would make his parents very happy. But the sanctuary would make Lucky happy, which was a distinction he was only now grasping, appreciating, as a grown man who wanted something as much as he'd ever wanted anything before. And again, he thought of Rachel.

Jenny frowned. "What is it, Luck?"

"An animal sanctuary," he said.

They stared at him. And then a few of his cousins smiled. And then one of his uncles nodded. One by one, they began looking at each other as the idea started sinking in.

Jack hooked his thumbs in his belt loops, looking curious. "Go on…"

"Sleigh Bell is struggling," Lucky said matter-of-factly. "We can't keep going like this. Without the free advertising this month, we would've been sunk by New Year's. On top of that, Grandma and Grandpa are going to retire soon. That leaves us to run the place. Or hire out. Which means entrusting the farm to an outsider. Not to say it can't be done—we have a lot of great hands. Pete, for one. But it wouldn't be the same. There's no getting around that. Do we *want* to hire out?"

It was an important question and the first hurdle he was going to have to clear if the idea of the sanctuary were to really stick. They all had to agree on this.

After a few seconds, everyone looked over at his grandparents, who were sitting quietly, taking it all in. They glanced at each other, then at Lucky, their gazes sharp.

"We've talked about this, son," his grandpa said. "We want the farm to stay under the supervision of the family. The business is separate. But when it comes to the land, it's your inheritance. It's either run by an Elliott, or we sell and give you all your share to hopefully enrich your lives with, and do some good in our community. That's the deal."

Lucky nodded. They'd always said you needed to know when to quit while you were ahead. A valuable lesson they were continuing to teach on this cold December evening with their own legacy hanging by a thin, sparkling thread, like a spider web in the sun.

He looked at the rest of his family in the room, and they all gazed back.

"Let's take a vote," he said. "All in favor of running Sleigh Bell ourselves, raise your hands."

Slowly, hands started rising into the air. One by one, every single person in the room had their hand up.

Lucky felt a stirring of excitement in his chest. "Okay. That's good. Unanimous agreement will be really important from here on out."

Jenny sat forward, the red sequins on her dress catching the light. "What kind of sanctuary are we talking about? I just toured one with my girlfriend last fall. It was for birds that couldn't be released back into the wild."

"I know the one you're talking about," Lucky said. "Take Flight. They have some world-renowned avian vets on staff."

From across the room, his father watched him, his expression unreadable.

"You're not thinking wild animals?" This, from Jesse.

"No, no," Lucky said. "This would be a sanctuary for elderly donkeys and horses. Montana is full of them. Animals that are past their prime and are no longer useful. At least to their current owners. They're hard to place because of their age or health issues. Mostly they just get sent to slaughter houses, and nobody notices."

He took a deep breath. Jenny was biting the inside of her cheek, her eyes bright. He was getting through. At least to some of them.

"But they're not throw-away animals," he continued. "We all know that. Dave and Betsy aren't something to be discarded just because their joints ache or they're slower than they used to be. They've worked hard for us. They deserve this kindness. A place to rest, where they're valued and loved."

The room was silent for a few seconds as this settled. They were a farm family. A tough family, hardened by years of working their land. But compassion ran deep in the Elliott veins. Their animals were the lifeblood of the farm. They all knew it. Without them, Sleigh Bell would be 80 acres of grass and trees. The donkeys had given them a livelihood, a foundation to build on.

"I think this is the best idea ever," Jenny said. "I'm in."

"Wait, wait, wait," Jack said, holding up a hand. "How would it work? Where would we get the money to run this thing? *Who* would run this thing?"

The first question was easy enough. It was the second one Lucky had been dreading the most.

"Well," he said, "in order to become official, we'd need to come up with a mission statement and bylaws, articles of incorporation. We'd want to be tax exempt, so those things would be required as the first step. Then we'd need to become accredited."

Jack nodded slowly.

"And then the real work." Lucky said. "We'd need to come up with several fundraisers a year, which shouldn't be too hard, since Marietta locals have a history of pitching in. But we'd also have to hold tours, get community members on board to sponsor animals, that kind of thing. We'd need someone in public relations to help, someone in website design. And a good vet to volunteer their services."

He looked over at his dad, who gazed back, stony faced.

"We'd also have a couple of directors," he continued. "To run the place."

His father crossed his arms over his chest. "And that'd be you?"

Lucky steeled himself against that intense gaze. The gaze so familiar from his boyhood. "Yes, Dad," he said evenly. "Patrick would run it with me."

Patrick stood then, in a show of support. He knew this was Lucky's battle to fight, but as a partner in the sanctuary, it was his baby, too.

"Yes, sir," Patrick said. "I'm on board."

Lucky's dad looked over at his nephew. "And you'd work at the fire department at the same time?"

"Yes, sir. I can do both. I'd be part-time at the sanctuary, and Lucky would be full time."

At that, the older man looked sharply back at his son. "What about graduate school?"

Lucky knew that everyone had questions, something to say, or comment on. Their energy was almost palpable. But at the sound of his dad's voice, the room fell quiet. So quiet that you could hear a pin drop.

He swallowed hard, his tongue thick and dry in his mouth. "I wouldn't go back to school."

At that, a distinct color crept up his father's neck. His mom looked worried. They still thought he was going to fuck his life up. It was obvious. Same old Lucky.

"And throw it all away?" his dad said. "Waste your undergraduate degree?"

"It's not a waste," Lucky said. "It'd help me run the sanctuary. All those classes under my belt would help me take care of the animals."

"But you won't be a vet. Which a way to help the most."

"It's your way of helping. And it's a great way. But it's not the way I want."

"Lucky," his mother said. "This is a wonderful thing you want to do. But you have to know it's a risk."

He nodded. "Yes. I know that."

"But you're willing to do it anyway," his father said.

"If the family is behind me, yes. I am."

"And what happens if you fail?"

His father's eyes were dark. The insinuation was as thick and uncomfortable as a wool blanket between them. *What if you fail?* What if, despite all the good intentions in the world, he crashed and burned? Then what?

"I don't plan on failing," he said, working to keep his voice even, and the anger and pain pushed to the side where they needed to stay. For everyone's sake.

"But what if you do? What about all those animals you want to help? Where the hell would they go then?"

He gritted his teeth and forced himself to stay rooted in place.

"And the land?" his dad continued. "The inheritance your grandparents worked so hard to leave you? It's not just yours. It's your brothers', your cousins'. If you go under, the farm could go under. You have to know that."

"Uncle Hank," Patrick said, his voice even. "With all due respect, I don't believe that'll happen. I think Lucky has what it takes to do this."

Lucky's father turned on him. "You're willing to bet your savings? Because I know that's what you'd be putting into this thing."

Patrick nodded. "Yes, sir. I'm willing to bet it all."

"We know the risks, Dad," Lucky said. "But we also know the rewards. This could be a great legacy for Sleigh Bell. Something we could all be proud of."

"We're already proud of it," his dad said flatly. "What we want is a secure future for you kids."

At that, another wave of silence settled over the room. This one felt significant. The big grandfather clock in the corner ticked the seconds off dutifully. Jenny shifted on the couch and her spiky heels scraped over the hard wood floor. Someone cleared their throat.

"Ellen, we'd better get going if we want to stop by the chocolate shop before the auction," his dad said, holding out a hand to help her off the loveseat. Then, he turned back to Lucky. "We can talk about this later. You'll probably end up doing what you want, anyway. But I hope you'll at least listen to reason."

Lucky bit back a reply. It would've been defensive, and he didn't want to argue.

His mom got up and gave him an anxious look. When it came to believing in him, he knew his parents wanted to. But it wasn't the same as actually digging deep and finding the faith to trust him. It was a jagged pill to swallow, and Lucky realized, at that moment, he might always be a gamble where they were concerned.

They said goodbye and told everyone they'd see them at the auction. Nobody seemed to take a breath until the front door closed.

They all looked at each other, the clock ticking in the background.

Jenny sat forward, her auburn hair falling over one

shoulder. "Well, I still think this is a great idea." She glanced around. "We all love the farm. But none of us are willing or able to help run it when Grandma and Grandpa retire, right?"

Every person in the room murmured in agreement. No one really wanted to admit not wanting to work the farm. But Lucky couldn't blame them. They had their own lives. And just because they didn't want to now, or couldn't now, didn't mean that wouldn't change in the future.

"And Lucky and Patrick are proposing something that'll keep it going. For a while, at least. I'd love to see what happens with this. Who's willing to give it a shot?"

"If anyone can do this, Lucky can," Jack said. "I'm in."

"Hell, count me in too," Jesse said.

Jake ran his big hands over his thighs. "You know I'm up for anything, little brother."

"Grandma? Grandpa?" Jenny said. "Your blessing?"

His grandmother's gaze settled on Lucky. "We want what you kids want. But we agree—if anyone can do this, it's Lucky. We'll support it and proudly."

Jenny grinned. Then held up her eggnog. "For Dave and Betsy, then."

A dozen more glasses rose in the air. "For Dave and Betsy," everyone said in unison.

Lucky's family was lining up behind him. And that felt really, really good. He wanted to raise his glass, too, but despite everything, his heart was heavy. Without his parents there, the whole thing felt bittersweet.

He forced a smile and nodded. "For the donkeys."

Chapter Seventeen

LUCKY HELD THE lobby door open for Rachel, and she smiled, walking through. Her heels clicked on the floor as she loosened her scarf and looked around in awe.

The Graff was always beautiful during the holidays. But tonight it was showing off—twinkling yellow lights were draped around the polished staircase banister. Glittering silver stars hung from the ceiling, catching the light as they twisted back and forth. Four huge Christmas trees towered in every corner, and the entire place smelled like pine. The entrance to the ballroom beckoned with soft lighting and music. A few of the decorated trees were visible from where she stood, and they were spectacular. She couldn't wait to see Sleigh Bell's finished entry.

"Oh, wow," she breathed. "This might be the loveliest thing I've ever seen."

Lucky leaned down and kissed her. "Not quite the loveliest."

Her cheeks warmed as she gazed up at him. But he seemed subdued tonight, not nearly himself. There was a hint of sadness in his eyes that worried her. She knew he'd talked to his family before picking her up to head to the auction, and they'd all agreed to support the sanctuary. She thought he'd be over the moon. But there was something he wasn't telling her, it was obvious.

She began unbuttoning her wool pea coat and watched him steadily. He looked so handsome in his baby blue dress shirt and pinstriped tie. He wore a pair of dark-washed jeans and cowboy boots and smelled good enough to eat. But the expression on his face…

"What's wrong, Lucky?" she asked.

"Nothing's wrong."

People walked past, filing into the ballroom in a steady stream. The rest of his family was already there, and she was excited about meeting them. There were so many Elliotts, she could barely keep them all straight. But she couldn't relax until she knew what was going on. Until he trusted her with it.

"Lucky…" This time she said it softer and stepped close. "Please tell me. Aren't you happy about the sanctuary?"

"I'm happy."

"Then what?"

Sighing, he put his hands in his pockets. "I'm happy. I am."

"But?"

"I'm glad my family thinks I can do this," he said slowly. "But I was hoping my parents would think so too."

She frowned. "What'd they say?"

"The usual. I need to play it safe. The future is too important to mess up…"

Her heart sank. She knew this had been his worst fear

going in. And that no matter what happened from this day on, no matter how successful he was at what he chose to do, it would always be part of his fabric.

"They'll come around," she said. "They'll see how great this sanctuary is going to be, and how utterly brilliant you and Patrick are going to be running it. You'll see."

He smiled, and her heart fluttered like a newly hatched butterfly. He did this to her. Love, in all its complexity, had never felt this raw, this beautiful in her life.

"I don't know," he said. "I hope you're right."

She stood on her tiptoes and gave him a kiss on his cheek. It was rough with stubble—warm and tempting. Before she could help it, she imagined that stubble rubbing against her naked belly, and felt a wave of desire wash over her.

"I know I'm right," she said, wanting more than anything for him to believe it. For him to know how amazing he was in every way. If only he could see himself the way everyone else did. But at the same time, she knew what haunted Lucky was beyond her reach right now. What haunted him went back years and years and was born on the afternoon he'd almost lost his life.

The expression in his eyes softened, just as the lights in the ballroom dimmed a few yards away. The auction was going to start soon. And she was going to sit beside him, her hand in his, and watch as their farm's tree raised money for charity. She'd never felt the Christmas spirit take hold of her like it had tonight. And that had everything to do with Lucky.

"Come on," he said, wrapping an arm around her waist. "Jenny can't wait to meet you."

"THANKS FOR COMING out tonight, folks!" the auctioneer said, leaning into the mic and making it squelch. "And Merry Christmas from all of us here at Mistletoe and Montana! Don't forget to stop by the refreshment table for some champagne and chocolates from our very own Sage Carrigan at the Copper Mountain Chocolate Shop. The dancing is about to kick off, so stick around!"

The room erupted in applause, and the live band began playing *Jingle Bell Rock*. Rachel smiled over at Lucky, her program tucked underneath her arm as she clapped. It had been a successful evening by anyone's standards. Overall, the decorated trees had raised close to twenty-five thousand dollars for Marietta General. Folks from all over Montana had shown up and had given back in a big way. Sleigh Bell's donkey-themed tree had brought in over two thousand on its own, and Rachel kept thinking of all the people that would help. She was proud of Marietta, proud of this community. And proud of Lucky's family, who had such a long and colorful history here.

"Well," Lucky said. "That's a wrap."

His cousin Jenny reached over to take Rachel's hand. "I'm so glad you came tonight, Rachel. Are you meeting us for dinner?"

Rachel beamed. "Absolutely."

"We'll save you a spot, okay?"

"See you in a few," Lucky said.

The rest of his family waved as they left the ballroom, weaving in between the lit trees. She'd seen his cousin Patrick, had met his brothers, a couple of his uncles, and one aunt. And she'd talked to his parents, whom she'd liked right away. His mother was warm and chatty, and his father was quiet, but friendly. There was a sharp intelligence in his eyes that made her think he was probably evaluating every situation, every person he came in contact with.

Lucky had said he was a talented vet, and it wasn't hard to see why. She could also see that, if he were her dad, she'd want to please him, too. She thought of her own father, who didn't seem to care what she did, and felt a pang of sadness. Lucky had issues with his folks, and she had issues with hers. Different issues, same lingering doubt. Something they had in common.

Standing, they waited for the packed room to clear a little. Lucky put his hand on the small of her back, and she felt the subtleness of his claim, the heat of his hand through her dress. She noticed the glances of several young women walking past, curious, maybe a tiny bit jealous. Who wouldn't be? He was gorgeous.

He leaned down, and she felt his warm breath on the back of her neck. "Have I told you lately how beautiful you are?"

She smiled. "When you picked me up tonight."

"Well, you are. Beautiful."

The band slowed, and goosebumps rose along her arms

as they eased into "I'll Be Home For Christmas." Her favorite song from a childhood spent loving the holidays. Being lonesome for her dad. Clearly wishing at seven years old that she could step inside the sweet perfection of an advent calendar and close the tiny cardboard door behind her. All of a sudden, those memories were so vivid, that her eyes began to sting. The nostalgia so thick, that Lucky could probably see it etched all over her face.

She took his hand. "Dance with me?"

Squeezing her fingers, he led her onto the dance floor where about a dozen couples were already swaying in each other's arms. He pulled her close, and she went with the ease of a woman who was in love.

She lay her head against his chest and felt the steady thudding of his heartbeat against her cheek. They fit together so perfectly, sometimes she wondered if they hadn't been molded from the same clay. Two pieces of a delicate puzzle meant to find each other all these years later.

He pressed his lips to the top of her head, and she closed her eyes.

"I always thought this song was about Christmas," she said, opening them again to gaze at the twinkling trees across the room. "But it's more than that. I guess I didn't realize it until just now."

He was quiet for a few seconds, as if thinking it over. "I think it's really about finding your way home again," he finally said. "To the things that matter."

Yes, she thought. *That.*

After a minute, the music slowed and softened, coming

to a gentle end. Everyone clapped and whistled as the band eased into another song, this one faster, with a heavier beat.

Lucky leaned down and kissed her temple. "Ready?" he asked.

Nodding, she slipped her hand into his and followed him off the floor. They made their way through the crowd that was gathered at the dessert table and toward the door. People smiled and nodded as they walked past, some of them commented on the podcast, or asked about Sleigh Bell and Don and Loretta. Rachel warmed. It felt good to be associated with this family, with all their vibrancy and goodness. In a way, she felt like she was living out the words of the song. Like she was coming home again. Was it possible that what she'd always longed for had been right here in Marietta all along?

"Lucky Elliott?"

They turned to see an older man walking toward them. Handsome, graying hair, with a small paunch hanging over his belt buckle. He wore a western shirt, and a tie with a turquoise stone and leather tassels. He looked familiar. Nodding at her, he held out a hand to Lucky.

"Roger Steele, Mountain View Properties. You're a hard man to track down."

Lucky shook it, looking uneasy. She knew why. Mountain View Properties was a Bozeman-based company with a reputation for buying up land to build golf courses and hotels on. Lavish ones. They'd just opened a resort in Helena, and an up-and-coming country singer had been on hand for the ribbon-cutting ceremony. She'd read about it in the *Marietta Courier.*

"Consider me tracked," Lucky said. He sounded guarded. Rachel didn't know if Roger Steele would pick up on that, but she did. "This is Rachel O'Rourke."

The older man shook her hand. His thick fingers were rough, weathered. "Ma'am. It's an honor. I've been listening to your show. It's a treasure."

"Thank you, Mr. Steele."

"Roger, please." He turned back to Lucky. "You look like you're headed out?"

"We are. Family dinner."

"Ahh. Big family, I hear. The Elliotts are legendary in this county."

"I don't know about legendary, but we've been around a while."

"And that farm is a beauty. I have a sister who lives past you on the highway. Eagle Crest Road? I've driven by so many times, I've lost count. Gorgeous country."

Lucky nodded. Rachel stepped close and hooked her arm in his. This man had stopped Lucky for a reason. They all knew it. But what that reason was exactly remained to be seen.

The live music thumped in Rachel's chest. She waited, holding her breath.

"Look, Lucky," Roger Steel said, raising his voice above the band. "I usually shoot straight from the hip, and I don't want to keep you from that dinner, so I'll just say it."

Rachel could feel Lucky's bicep flex a little, like he was bracing himself.

"I listened to the First Kiss episode featuring your grandparents."

He and Rachel looked at each other.

"It was touching," he continued. "I know Sleigh Bell Farm has been in your family for a century."

"That's right."

"And it's an important part of your heritage, as it should be."

"Right again."

Roger Steele lowered his head, his eyes growing flinty. "But I know Don and Loretta won't be able to run it much longer. Not at their age."

Lucky stiffened at that.

"Oh, I'm not saying they're not capable, son. It's obvious they are, or they wouldn't have done the phenomenal job they have over the years. But it's a lot of work. Anyone who's lived on a ranch knows that. I'm a farm boy myself."

"What's this all about, Mr. Steele?"

"Roger."

"Roger," Lucky said evenly. "What's this all about?"

"I just want to put a bug in your ear. Just something to think about."

Lucky waited, his jaw working.

"I don't know if you and your family have thought about selling recently. I'm not talking about the house, of course," He rushed to add this part, like he expected to be cut off any second. "But the acreage. It's a lot of land, and it's prime Montana real estate."

Rachel watched Lucky. To her surprise, he stayed quiet while the other man went on. There was an expression on his face that she couldn't read, and her chest tightened.

"I could promise you, Lucky, that we'd honor that land. Build something beautiful, tasteful. And you could even keep the carriage ride business going there if that's what you wanted. Keep the home, the barn, and some surrounding land. Totally up to your family. I just know realistically, in this day and age, that a farm like Sleigh Bell can drain folks. Take more than they have to give. Sometimes it's just better to know when to walk away. To know when it's time."

Rachel still had no idea what Lucky was thinking. Apparently Roger Steele didn't know either, because he leaned slightly forward. Then spoke in low tones, so nobody else who passed by would hear.

"I could also promise you that my company would be prepared to set you up for life. Give your grandparents the retirement they deserve. Give a young man like you a solid future."

Those things could be considered presumptuous. Very, since Roger Steele didn't know Lucky or his family, or anything about how they wanted to proceed with the farm. But, at the same time, Marietta was a small town, and it didn't take too much digging to expose someone's vulnerability. And that was exactly what he'd just done.

Lucky's expression had changed from quiet skepticism to a certain kind of pained realization. An offer like this would be hard to turn down under the best of circumstances. But when it landed in his lap at a time with so much perceived risk about the sanctuary, it was probably more tempting than she knew.

Plus, what would the rest of the Elliotts think of this?

She realized she might be witnessing the death of his dream before it even took its first breath. An arrow straight to the heart. And all of a sudden, she had the overwhelming urge to dump a cup of punch down the front of Roger Steele's nice western shirt.

As if reading her mind, he turned and smiled at her. All even white teeth against tanned skin. Charming. But it was a calculated charm, she could tell. A man like this didn't wear the expensive boots and flashy Rolex for nothing. He'd earned them. And he wanted people to know he'd earned them.

"Miss O'Rourke, it was a pleasure meeting you."

"You, too," she said. But it wasn't a pleasure. It had been horrible. Five minutes of pure horrible.

He turned to Lucky with the same smile. As if they'd known each other since dirt. "Here's my card, son. Give me a call, and we can talk. Maybe after the holidays? I'm headed to Aspen with my wife, but after that, I'll be around, and I'll buy you a beer, okay?"

Lucky took the card and shook the other man's hand looking pale and a little shell shocked. Absorbing it. Swallowing it down. Trying not to choke on it.

"Thanks," he said. "I'll think it over."

"That's all I ask. Merry Christmas, kids."

And before they could answer, he was walking out the door, leaving a faint cloud of cologne behind him.

"Well," Lucky said. "That was weird."

Rachel watched him. "So…what are you thinking?"

"Honestly?"

She nodded.

"I have no idea. I'll have to tell my grandparents, the rest of the family. They'll need to know."

The band had moved on to "Have Yourself a Merry Little Christmas." The lights had dimmed even more in the ballroom, making the surrounding Christmas trees sparkle with a heavenly luster. Christmas had officially come to Marietta. The entire hotel was under its spell.

"Have you ever thought about selling?" she asked, hooking her arm in his again. Suddenly, she was tired. Emotional. Maybe the farm symbolized more to her than she'd realized. Maybe it represented not only a dream, but a future with Lucky as well. Because if he was able to put his faith in the sanctuary, a relative unknown, maybe he would put his faith in her, too. In whatever was growing between them. Love and faith, operating side by side, could lead to beautiful things.

"We have," he said. "I don't think anyone really wants to, but we would. If the time was right. And maybe if the circumstances were right."

He looked down at her, his expression unreadable again. He was somewhere else now. Somewhere she couldn't follow.

Putting his hand over hers, he squeezed, smiling in a way that said he wasn't prepared to talk about it anymore. At least not tonight.

"Hungry?" he asked, his voice low.

She smiled back, but felt a tickle of apprehension in her lower belly. "Starving," she said.

Chapter Eighteen

L UCKY LED THE little black horse out to the middle of the paddock and unsnapped the lead rope from his bright red halter. The color looked good on him. It popped against his fuzzy, ebony coat.

Dreamer shook his head, then stood there, looking at Lucky. His forelock hung over one eye, and his ears were pricked curiously. He was a precocious thing and smart as a whip. He was a good horse, and Lucky was getting attached. Something he'd been fighting, but wasn't sure why.

It had finally stopped snowing, at least for a while, leaving six new inches of fluff across town. Christmas was only a few days away, and his family was busy doing some last-minute shopping, baking, and wrapping. The rest of his cousins were coming in today, and they'd be having Christmas Eve dinner at the farm day after tomorrow.

As for Lucky, the hours after the auction had been some of the longest of his life. His conversation with Roger Steele kept replaying in his head. Actually, it hadn't been so much a conversation as a bombshell that Lucky had to dig his way out from under. The suggestion of selling the farm had left him with questions, of course. Significant ones. What would his family want to do with this? What did *he* want to do with this?

But the thing that bothered him the most was what his dad would think of it. What would he think the most responsible thing was? Lucky knew the answer to that. He'd known his entire life. And, hell. Maybe his dad was right. Graduate school was a sure bet. Running the carriage ride business without the overhead of keeping the farm up, was a sure bet. The sanctuary was not a sure bet, and that was the monkey on his back.

As the hours had passed the other night, he'd grown more and more quiet. Over dinner, Rachel kept looking over at him, her features drawn. She'd known right away where he was going with this. And it worried her.

He stepped back from Dreamer now, his boots crunching in the snow, and climbed up on the paddock gate. He settled on the cold metal bar and shoved his hands deep into his heavy Carhartt jacket pockets. The horse watched him, trying to decide what his new master wanted of him, then sighed deeply, his breath billowing from his nostrils in a silver cloud.

"Go on," Lucky said.

Dreamer didn't move.

"Go on," Lucky said again, harsher than he meant. "Get."

At the tone, the horse tossed his head, then trotted out the paddock opening into the pasture.

Lucky watched him with tightness in his chest. If he didn't go ahead with the sanctuary, would he be letting animals like this one down? Animals that had no other place to be? Or would he be letting them down if he opened the sanctuary, only to have to close it again because there wasn't enough money to keep it running? If they had to close, the animals in their possession would have to go. And it would have to be a quick decision *where* they went. It wasn't a good scenario and one his father had rightly pointed out. They'd all seen ventures like this fail. Too many times to count.

He thought about Rachel again and how she'd felt moving underneath him the other night. How perfect that had been. They were planning on a date tomorrow; *National Lampoon's Christmas Vacation* was showing at the movie theater. But he was hesitant. There was a part of him that wanted to leave things with her like they'd been at the auction –unflawed, brimming with promise. Before they got screwed up. Before he was the one to screw them up. He could always come back for her. After graduation. After his life was in order and his future was solid. If she'd have him, he'd come back.

He watched Dreamer canter into the pasture, kicking up the snow underneath his hooves. He held his tail high, and it waved like a weather-beaten flag behind him. He looked wild right then, free.

And Lucky envied him.

RACHEL WALKED BESIDE Lucky, their breath crystalizing on the night air. The shops were still open, their warm, yellow lights spilling onto the sidewalk. The window displays were spectacular, and it seemed, everywhere she looked, Christmas was gazing back.

She loved this time of year. Even though her father had been away most of her childhood, she and her mom always made the best of it. Baking cookies and watching movies in front of a crackling fire. This Christmas wouldn't be any different.

She was even thinking of asking Lucky over later in the afternoon. She knew his family was in town, and they had plans. But she'd bought him a present and wanted to see him open it on Christmas Day. It was a plaque for his new office that she'd had engraved. It read, *Lucky Elliott, Director*. And next to that, were two small donkeys pulling a sleigh.

Rachel could hardly wait. But he was quiet tonight, pensive. When they'd left her apartment for the movie, she'd tried to lighten the mood with some *Christmas Vacation* quotes by the ever-clueless Clark Griswold. But Lucky would only smile, looking straight ahead. She'd finally given up and put her hands in her pockets, knowing he was deep in thought. Wrestling with something significant.

"I called Roger Steele today," he said suddenly, startling her.

They were just passing the Graff, with its big, frosted windows. She could smell the food cooking from inside the bar.

She slowed. "Oh?"

He nodded. His profile was strong and rugged in the shadows. Handsome, as always. But there was something different about him tonight—something resolute. It was possible she was reading into this. But she didn't think so. Ever since Roger Steele pulled that glossy business card out of his pocket and handed it over, she'd hoped this moment wouldn't materialize. Had hoped with all her heart. But, at the same time, she'd known it might.

Lucky slowed, too. Then came to a stop and faced her. "Yes."

"And?"

"It'd be more than I thought, Rachel."

She raised her brows, but had to bite her lip to keep it from quivering. She couldn't help it. The disappointment that washed over her was all-consuming. If someone had asked her to describe what it felt like, she wouldn't have been able to. It just felt *sad*. Like she was losing something she'd never really had to begin with.

"How much more?" she asked.

"Enough to take care of our grandparents when they can't take care of themselves anymore. Enough to send my younger cousins to college. Enough not to have to worry about the future."

She watched him. He'd always wanted to do the right thing. And now, here was a gilded offer from a man who was offering up redemption, peace, security. All the things Lucky craved.

"You've talked to Patrick and the rest of your family?" she asked.

"Not yet, but I'm going to. We'd have to decide together, of course."

"And the sanctuary?"

He frowned and shook his head. "We could lose the animals. We could lose the farm eventually. We could lose everything."

"But you wouldn't. You have to know that in your heart."

At that, he looked up sharply. "I don't know that."

"You believed it the other day. You believed it then, and now this."

She was pushing, and she shouldn't be. But she loved him. She knew that now. And his dream was that sanctuary. Maybe even his destiny. It was killing her softly standing there on that frozen sidewalk watching him blow it from his palms like dust.

"I'll always admire you for reaching so high for what you want, Rachel," he said. "Always. But we're different. I can't just dismiss my reality like that."

She narrowed her eyes. "I'm dismissing my reality?"

"I didn't mean it like that. But you don't have as much on the line as I do."

"No," she said. "That's true. I don't have someone offering me money to quit." She immediately wished she could bite the words back. Together, they were screwing this conversation up faster than it was taking to have it.

His eyes flashed, and his lips formed a hard line before he spoke again. "Yes, someone's offering us money. But it's not about the money. It's about the security."

"I'm sorry," she said. "I didn't mean that. But what about *you*, Lucky? What about what's best for you? You're always thinking of everyone else, what will make them happy. But what if you're doing what you think is making them happiest with *you*?"

He crossed his arms over his chest. "Meaning my parents."

"Yes. But meaning everyone else, too."

"I'm not going to lie and say I don't think about that. I do."

She stepped forward. "I want you to be happy doing what's best for you. You deserve that. Don't you think success will follow if you lead with your heart?"

He laughed bitterly. "That's what I'm talking about. I'd let myself start to think that. And it's unrealistic. There are just too many unknowns, too many variables. Wanting something and loving the idea...having the best intentions aren't enough."

"What about me?"

He paused at that. "What?"

"What about what you said about me?" Rachel asked softly. "About me following my dreams with the podcast? Have you thought it was unrealistic this whole time?"

"Of course not. You know that's not true."

"I don't know that. Because you've led me to believe we were alike. Fundamentally. That we were both dreamers. You made me think you believed in me, that I could do this. But if starting a sanctuary is too much of a stretch for a vet student, then a waitress launching a podcast that will pay the bills is *definitely* a stretch."

He looked conflicted, pissed, ready to walk away.

"I never said anything to make you feel less than, Rachel," he finally answered back. His voice was hoarse, strained. "Ever."

She felt the sting of tears, but told herself she wasn't going to cry. Not now. Maybe later, with Lucy's warm little body tucked in her arms and a pint of Ben and Jerry's on the coffee table. But not while he was standing there looking at her with such obvious misunderstanding. Such frustration. He didn't get it. Maybe he never would.

"Don't you see, Lucky?" she asked. "Don't you see what I'm saying?"

He watched her, quiet.

"It's not what you *said* to make me feel like you believed in me. It's what you *did*. You going after what you wanted deep, deep down, despite everything, despite how you worried it would be perceived by your folks…meant that maybe I'd inspired you. It meant that what I was doing with the podcast made sense to you on some level. And I've never inspired anyone before. I've never done anything special. Even more than the podcast, I was proud that I had a part in that."

There was a flicker in his eyes then, a spark of something she'd seen before. And then it was gone. A wall rose slowly in its place. She knew that he'd protect himself from this moment fiercely. He'd spent years anticipating it and, as strongly as she felt for him, as much as she wanted to knock that wall down with her bare hands, she was no match for the survival instinct that had gotten him through every single day up until this one.

"So, you're saying I've let you down," he said. "I've failed you."

Her heartbeat slowed. "You never failed me. You're not failing anyone. And as disappointed as I feel right now, a lot of this is on me. I expected something different, but I'll readjust. You're not going to end up breaking all the people you care for, Lucky. You're just not."

"I'm not. Because I'm going to do what's right. What's best."

It had started snowing again. Big, soft flakes fell all around them. Soon, their footprints would be completely covered. As if they'd never stood there at all.

"And what's right is going back to school?" she asked, not wanting the answer, but knowing it just the same.

He nodded. "Yes," he said. "I'm going back to school."

"And us?" She thought she knew the answer to that, too.

There was silence again. The snow drifted down, down, falling onto the pine trees surrounding them. Against the shop windows and cars that were huddled in their parking spots along the street. It was a winter wonderland, a Christmas dream come true. But Rachel could only feel the ache in her throat. The pain in her chest, as if it were being ripped in two.

"I'd be going back for you, too, Rachel," he said quietly. "To be the best man I can be for you. You deserve that."

She couldn't say anything. She was afraid, if she did, she'd cry, and she didn't want that. She didn't want him staying out of guilt.

"After Christmas, I'm going back to Bozeman," he said. "In time for next semester. Get my old job back. Pick up where I left off."

She watched him steadily. He had snow on his shoulders now. In his hair and eyelashes.

"So, this is it," she managed.

"For now," he said. "It has to be. But I'll be back."

She nodded. Okay. So, this was her new reality. She'd continue loving him, but from afar. As long as her heart would allow. She'd still believe in happy endings, even if it was by telling other peoples' stories. She was a dreamer. She'd always be a dreamer, for better or worse.

Burying his hands in his pockets, he hunched his shoulders against cold. The Christmas wreaths on the light poles clinked in the breeze. A car passed with reindeer antlers tied to its grill, and a couple walked by, balancing brightly wrapped packages in their arms.

He looked at her through the snow falling between them. Then he glanced down, as if thinking of what to say. She waited, her jaw aching with the effort of keeping her teeth from chattering.

When he looked back, his eyes were bright. He hadn't been thinking of what to say. He'd been composing himself.

"No matter what happens," he said. "I'll always..."

At that, his voice broke. Just the smallest bit. He didn't go on.

She stepped forward, toward him, toward his warmth and magnetism. Toward something she chose to believe blindly in. Maybe they didn't have a future. But they had tonight. They had this moment right here.

She took his hand in hers. "I know," she said. "I love you, too, Jim."

Chapter Nineteen

LUCKY SAT ON the top step of his grandparents' porch with Stitch's head on his lap. It was a beautiful Christmas Eve, the kind that looked like a movie set. Snow fell through the darkness, and a thick blanket of it cloaked the farm. Except for the low Christmas music coming from inside, there was a peaceful silence that he'd been craving since telling his family about Roger Steele's offer over dinner.

Stitch sighed deeply, his little body pressed close. Lucky rubbed his ears, looking out toward the barn where Pete was taking care of the animals tonight. Everyone was bedded down in warm, clean straw. Soft light spilled out onto the snow, making the winter shadows retreat toward the tree line and dark, rolling pastures beyond.

God, he loved it out here. But the last few days had filled him with an unimaginable sadness at the thought of leaving it. Of leaving Marietta. And of leaving Rachel.

Picturing how she'd looked the other night, standing there like her heart was breaking, did things to him that were as painful as anything he'd ever experienced. He'd needed some time. Time to absorb it all, time to come to terms with what was happening; to his future, to a new love that had taken him completely by surprise. To his dreams that had just begun to unfold their wet, fragile wings, only for him to force them away again. This time, maybe for forever.

The news that Roger Steele wanted to buy Sleigh Bell had settled over their family dinner in waves, quieting them all. It hadn't been the reaction he'd been expecting. When his aunts and uncles, cousins and brothers did start talking, it was hesitantly. As if they didn't quite believe it. Or didn't want to believe it.

Lucky's parents hadn't said a thing. He'd just looked up to see his father watching him with his cool blue eyes, his expression unreadable. Was he relieved? Happy that his son would be following in his footsteps?

Lucky had always wanted his father to be proud of the man he'd become. But tonight, for the very first time, that constant need for approval had taken a backseat to his own feelings of loss. Of so many things.

He'd sat at the old dining room table, unable to eat. And not hungry anyway. After a few minutes, he'd excused himself, saying he was going to make a phone call, and had walked out the front door with Stitch at his feet.

He'd ended up on the porch, sitting in the same spot he'd sat as a kid, thinking, in those weeks and months after the fire.

Stitch thumped his tail against the porch as the door opened with a squeak behind them. Lucky turned to see his grandmother walk out, a thick, red shawl wrapped around her shoulders. She looked tired tonight. She insisted on doing the Christmas cooking every year, but it was probably time to start changing that, too. Life changed. Change was the only constant.

She sat down on the other side of Stitch, her knees popping. Lucky caught the scent of her perfume, something she'd been wearing ever sense he could remember. He couldn't tell if it reminded him of the flowers she kept on the breakfast nook table or the brown sugar in her cookies. But she always smelled like home.

Smiling over at him now, she patted Stitch's head.

"What are you doing out here all by yourself?"

He ran his hands down his thighs. It was cold. Really cold. But the house had felt stifling, and he'd needed air.

"Just thinking."

"About?"

"Things."

She shook her head, watching him. "You think too much, Lucky. You always have."

After a minute, her gaze shifted toward the barn and the sounds of the animals settling for the night. There was a whinny, then another. Then, the slam of a stall door closing before the tack room light flickered off.

"Remember when you were little and you had that ratty brown stick horse? I can't think of its name. Betty? Bitsy?"

Lucky grinned. "Benny."

"*Benny.*" His grandmother slapped her knee. "That's it. You rode that thing everywhere. You were too small to ride the ponies like your brothers, so you just made do."

"I remember that. His ear fell off, and you sewed it back on."

She laughed. "Yes, I did. But we had to find it first. One of our mama kitties had it with her kittens. You were always with the babies. In fact, I don't think there's been a baby born on this farm that you haven't welcomed into the world."

He nodded, the memories so thick now, he could almost reach out and touch them. "The Welcome Wagon," he said. "That's what dad used to call me."

"He was so proud of you. Of how you were with the animals. He knew you were different, because he was, too."

Lucky watched her.

She smiled, the wrinkles in her face deepening. "It's in your blood. Your daddy, he chose to do something with his gift that we thought was the best thing at the time. The most responsible thing. And your grandpa and I were happy about that. But now…"

He waited. There was a change in her voice. A wavering.

"But now," she went on softly, "we know we probably made a mistake with him. We wanted so many things for our kids, for them not to have to work as hard as we did. To get an education and see the world differently. But now we see that your dad had dreams he gave up because of what we wanted."

Lucky sat there, dumbfounded. The fact that his father might've wanted to be something other than a vet had never occurred to him, never even entered his frontal lobe until right then.

"What kind of dreams?" he asked.

"Oh, I don't know. He wanted to be a ball player at one

point. Had a pretty good arm. The point is, he's been where you are, son. And he knows you're just wanting to please him. Like he wanted to please us. Life is funny like that. We end up repeating the same mistakes over and over, and with the people we love the most. All in the name of wanting them to be happy."

"You think Dad's unhappy?" Something else that never occurred to him. His father seemed content, in control of his life. Happiness always seemed like an afterthought for his parents. They seemed happy *enough.*

"I think he's a grown man who's still learning where his heart is. I think he loves deeply and expects a lot. He's a complicated person, but he's a good person. And he'd do anything for his kids. Anything."

Like walk through fire.

Lucky swallowed hard.

"You know," she continued, her voice low, "seeing you hurt as a boy nearly killed him. He almost didn't come through it."

"I know. I'm so sorry."

She turned to him. "You still think…"

He didn't trust himself to speak.

"Jim, he's always blamed himself."

At the sound of his given name, he lowered his head into his hands. Like when Rachel had said it the other night, he felt seen for the first time since he was ten years old. But did he really want to be seen? He'd always thought he had. But this felt jarring, painful. Too raw for comfort.

"He's never forgiven himself for not being out there with

you that day," his grandmother continued. "He knew you had the sparklers and wanted to play with them." She took a deep breath and exhaled slowly. "But it was an accident. A horrible, horrible accident. You carry enough of it with you for all of us. But I wish you'd let it go. I wish you'd forgive yourself. Maybe if you did, your dad would forgive himself, too."

"I don't know how, Grandma. I've tried."

She put her hand on his knee.

"If it was just the fire, or the barn…" he continued. His vocal cords felt dry and brittle. Like they might snap in half. "Or even losing the horses, that would be one thing. But it's changed me. I don't know how to be the person I want to be. With the animals. With everything."

"You already are that person. Everyone knows it but you. Rachel knows it, she feels it. And I think that's why you're pushing her away like this."

"I'm not pushing her away. Going back to school isn't pushing her away."

"Isn't it?" She studied him. "That sanctuary would force you to accept the love you've been denying yourself for a long time. From friends and family. From Rachel."

"And selling the farm would provide for the entire family."

"If that's the excuse you're trying to make…"

"I'm not making—"

He stopped short at the sound of footsteps in the darkness. They both looked up to see Pete jogging toward them, his breath coming in short, frosty puffs.

"Sorry to bother you, folks," the older man said. "But you'd better come out here, Lucky. There's something wrong with Betsy."

LUCKY KNEELED BESIDE the little donkey stretched out in the straw. Her breath was coming fast, and her eyes were glazed and hooded. He ran a hand down her neck, as Dave brayed from the neighboring stall.

Pete stood off to the side, scratching Dave's ears through the metal bars, trying to comfort him. "I know, Davey," he said. "Your girl isn't feeling well, is she?"

"Has she been off her feed?" Lucky asked.

"She ate fine yesterday. I was wondering if she might be a little colicky today. But she didn't eat a thing tonight, and then when I came back in from taking care of the horses, she'd gone down like this. Couldn't get her up."

Lucky frowned. This wasn't good. Donkeys were notoriously tough, and Dave and Betsy rarely showed signs of distress.

He had a baseline knowledge of equine sickness from college and his time on the farm, but he also knew this was serious and beyond him. If it was what he thought it was, they needed to move fast.

"Pete," he said. "Can you get my dad, please?"

"Sure thing, Luck."

Pete left him alone with Betsy as the snow continued falling in fat flakes outside the barn doors. Dave brayed again, breaking Lucky's heart. They were old and so bonded most people couldn't tell one from the other. They'd come to the farm as yearlings and had grown up together. Had grown up with Lucky. If something were to happen to Betsy tonight, if they were to lose her, Dave would grieve deeply. Maybe even get sick himself because of the stress. There was no way to explain to him what was happening or reassure him. He would only feel the acute loss, the emptiness of her presence in his life.

Lucky stroked Betsy's coat and looked up at Dave who had his fuzzy gray nose sticking through the bars. His big, dark eyes took them in. His nostrils flared, his velvety lips twitching as he breathed in Betsy's scent.

"I know, buddy," Lucky said. "She doesn't want to leave you, either."

The donkey's big ears rotated at the sound of his voice, and he didn't bray again.

It felt like a lifetime, but finally there was the sound of footsteps in the snow, low voices coming from outside.

And then his dad appeared with Pete by his side. He wore a heavy down jacket and had his medical bag slung over his shoulder. Since he was a large animal vet, he basically drove an ambulance, which had come in handy on more than one occasion. He'd once delivered a calf on the side of a desolate Montana highway. The owners had named it after him, an honor his friends still ribbed him about. Tonight, his face was bright red from the cold, his jaw covered in a rusty, five-o'clock shadow.

"Aww, Betsy," he said, as he unhooked the stall door and

stepped in. "We're not letting you go on Christmas Eve. So don't get any ideas."

Kneeling down beside Lucky, he patted his son's shoulder. A brief sign of affection from a man who didn't usually show much. Then he turned to Betsy, putting his hands on her, soothing her, assessing what might be wrong in a way so brilliant and quick, it was humbling to watch. He smelled faintly of aftershave, some beer on his breath from dinner. He smelled like his father, and right then, Lucky was so proud, it left him raw inside.

"Pete," his dad said.

"Yeah, boss?"

"I know your family's waiting, and you've stayed longer than you planned tonight."

Pete shook his head, getting ready to argue.

Lucky's dad looked up. "Go home. Enjoy Christmas Eve with Jill and the grandkids. I'll call you later, let you know how she is, okay?"

"Well, I couldn't leave old Betsy…"

"We'll take care of her. We're not going to let anything happen to her. Not tonight. Go."

The words were stern, but the tone they were spoken in was uncharacteristically tender. Hank Elliott was at his absolute best in moments like these. It was why he was such a good vet. He cared for the animals, but he also knew how to comfort their human friends, too. It was an important part of the job, at least as far as Lucky was concerned.

Pete hesitated for another few seconds, then nodded slowly, reluctantly. "Okay. But if you need me—"

"I know. We'll call. Go ahead, so you can make your church service, okay?"

"Okay, boss." He smiled at Lucky and touched the brim of his cowboy hat. "Merry Christmas."

"Merry Christmas to you, Pete," Lucky said.

And with that, Lucky and his dad were alone in the barn, the sick donkey lying between them. Dave had fallen silent and was now pacing back and forth in the next stall over. His hooves shuffled softly through the straw.

"She's definitely got colic," Lucky's dad said. "But the question is why. I think I might know…"

Lucky frowned, watching him. He thought he knew, too. It could be anything. She could've eaten something that was obstructing her bowels, or have an infection somewhere, or even a tumor. But he didn't think so. He'd seen a lot of ponies and donkeys throughout the years come down with hyperlipemia, a disease caused by too much fat in the blood. Betsy was a prime target because of her gender and age. The sickness came on quickly and was serious. The mortality rate was high, even when caught early and with proper treatment.

"She's running a fever," his dad said, putting the thermometer away. "I'll take some blood to make sure, but I think she's in for some trouble here."

Lucky moved forward and gently lifted the donkey's head into his lap. He stroked her face, her ears, while his dad drew blood. The vial slowly turned crimson as Betsy lay there listless.

His dad removed the needle and held the vial up to the light. "Cloudy," he said. "I'll test it, but I'm sure it's a negative energy balance."

"Should we try and feed her?" Lucky asked, knowing she was probably past this particular window, but also knowing with hyperlipemia, there was a checklist to follow. And the further down you got on it, the harder it was to get the animal to respond to treatment.

"She's too far along, too dehydrated. I think we'll have to use a tube."

Lucky nodded, stroking Betsy's nose. "Do you think she's going to make it?"

His dad patted her shoulder, his eyes bright. Brighter than Lucky had seen them in a long time. They all loved Betsy. She was a good donkey. The best.

"I don't know," he said. "We'll do everything we can. At least we can treat her here. Transporting her would be too stressful. Being away from Dave would probably be a deal breaker anyway."

Lucky gazed down at her. He hated this part of ranch life. But death went hand in hand with living. But he'd be here for it, no matter how hard it was.

He and his dad sat there in silence, the snow continuing to fall over the farm in its delicate, frozen beauty. Inside the house, the family would be having coffee by now, getting ready to exchange presents. They always opened one the night before Christmas—usually pajamas for the kids. The adults would be turning on a movie afterward, sitting around the fire while the little ones played in the family room. This would be Lucky's twenty-fifth Christmas in this house, with this family. And, even now, he wouldn't want to be anywhere else.

He felt the weight of his father's gaze and looked up. There was a vulnerability in his expression that Lucky wasn't used to. But he'd recognized it a few times. In the hospital after the fire, for one. When Jake had been gored by a bull two years ago, for another. It was a look of love. A look of worry. But there was pride there, too. That part was unmistakable.

"Seeing you out here…" his dad said.

Lucky waited, sensing something different in the older man's voice. Something meaningful. Something laced with promise.

"You have a gift, son." He continued slowly, "I used to think you should use it in a way that'd help you grow up, become a man."

Lucky watched him, his throat tight. The snow fell. Dave nosed in the straw a few feet away. And the barn seemed to be holding its breath.

"Now I know you've been grown for a while," his father continued. "I've just missed it because I still see you as that boy…who just wanted to be near the horses that day. You just wanted to be near them, that's all.

"Dad—"

"Let me say this. I need to say it." His father held up a hand, his eyes growing brighter. Bluer by the second, if that was possible. "I've been trying my damnedest to protect you. But, these last few days, I think I've finally realized something. I realized what I've really been doing is reining you in. Trying to control you. And there's no controlling someone's heart."

The world seemed to slow then. Lucky's arms felt heavy as the words sunk in. As they found their purchase in the deepest part of himself that had been waiting this whole time.

"Nobody wants to sell this farm," his father said. "Your mom and I have some reservations about the sanctuary, but we want you to try, okay?" He put an awkward hand on Lucky's shoulder and squeezed it for a second. "We believe in you, son."

Letting go, he stood, and hauled his bag up with him. Lucky lowered his gaze to Betsy again, unable to look anywhere else. He was too overwhelmed to speak. And he wouldn't have known what to say, anyway. He thought about Rachel. She believed in him, too. She'd seen in him things he hadn't wanted to see in himself. Things it took courage to accept, things that needed to be faced, confronted. And things that could be great, if he'd only let them take shape.

He saw his reflection in the donkey's eyes, before she blinked and closed them for a few long moments.

"I'll get the supplies," his dad said, opening the stall door. "We can take turns checking on her. It's going to be a long night."

Chapter Twenty

RACHEL SAT IN the cab of Bob's Ford F-250 with the heater blowing against her face. The wipers swooshed at the falling snow, clearing it, but all she could see out the windshield was darkness ahead. And snow. Lots and lots of snow.

Bob glanced over. "Nervous?"

He was wearing a red checkered hunter's cap with the flaps over his ears and bright red mittens to match. What didn't match was Bob and this ginormous truck. At all. But, like with everything else Bob, it was a contradiction in terms, and she had to smile at the sight of him behind the wheel. He could barely see over the top of it.

"Can you tell?"

"I can only hear those teeth clacking from over here," he said. "Take a deep breath."

"Thank you for picking me up. My car wouldn't have made it. Are you *sure* I wasn't interrupting anything? It's Christmas Eve."

"My *Miracle on 34th Street* marathon, but that can totally wait. At the moment, my mother is getting tipsy and arguing with my aunt about not following my granny's meringue recipe. So, yeah. I was available." He leaned forward to rub a clear spot in the windshield. "Oh my God. It's blizzarding out here."

"Is blizzarding a word?"

"If it's not, it should be. So, tell me again what he said?"

At the thought of the phone call she'd gotten from Lucky not half an hour ago, Rachel's heart squeezed. He'd told her he didn't have a lot of time to talk, that Betsy was sick. But that he wanted her to know he loved her. And he wanted to invite her and her mom to come out to the farm tomorrow on Christmas day. He had something to tell her.

She cradled her purse in her lap and tucked her chin into her scarf. "He didn't say much. Just that Betsy was sick and that we needed to talk."

"And that he's in love with you."

"And that."

"This is so *romantic*," Bob said. "Coming out here on Christmas Eve like this. It's just like one of your podcast episodes. Better even."

Grinning, he slowed the big truck when the Sleigh Bell sign came into view. They turned up the long drive, toward the old Victorian in the distance. Smoke curled from the chimney, promising a cozy fire inside. Christmas lights twinkled around the windows, and no less than ten vehicles sat in the driveway, their hoods covered with new snow.

But it was the barn where Rachel's gaze was drawn, as Bob guided the truck toward its half-open doors. Lucky's truck was out front. And so was another, that said *Henry Elliott, Large Animal Vet* on the side.

She hurt for Lucky and his family, who might be on the verge of losing something very special tonight. And she was overcome with a feeling of love for this place. Not just for the farm that had endeared itself to her over the last several weeks, but of Marietta itself. Of Montana, where stories like this were all too familiar. Farm life was hard. But these people were resilient. And more tender than they had a right to be.

Bob brought the truck to a stop, where it idled with a low rumble. "Here we are. You'll be okay?"

She unbuckled her seatbelt and leaned over to give him a hug. He smelled like peppermint. Of course he did.

"I'll be alright. Thanks again."

"Merry Christmas, Rach."

She gave him a quick peck on the cheek, then scooted back over, opened the heavy door, and hopped out. Pushing it closed again, she shivered in the cold night air. The snow was coming harder now, faster. But the farm was beautiful and dignified underneath the winter onslaught.

Bob backed out of the drive, and after a minute the big truck was reduced to just two glowing taillights through the storm.

Rachel turned toward the barn again. She didn't know how Lucky would react to seeing her tonight. She hadn't really thought it through. She'd only followed her heart.

She made her way toward the light coming from inside, her boots sinking into the knee-high drifts. And before she reached the big sliding doors, a shadow of a man appeared. The snow was coming so hard, she had to shield her eyes.

"Rachel?"

The sound of his voice made her pulse flutter behind her ears. All of a sudden, everything else fell away, and it was only Lucky.

"It's me," she said.

"What are you doing here?"

"I came to…" Suddenly, she didn't know what to say. *I came to tell you I love you? I came to sit with you through the night? To tell you I'll wait for you, however long it takes.*

It all fit. All of it. But she didn't know where to start. All the emotions from the last month were swirling around her heart in a tornado of color and warmth. Her throat ached as he walked out to meet her and pulled her into his arms.

He felt so solid. Smelled of hay and man. She lay her cheek against his rough work jacket and breathed him in.

"You're a sight for sore eyes," he said into her hair. "How'd you know?"

"How'd I know what?"

He pulled away and took her face in his hands. They were warm, despite the cold. Looking down at her, he smiled. "That you're all I've been thinking about tonight. You're all I've been wanting."

And then he kissed her. Rachel's heart beat like a drum inside her chest. Her blood roared through her veins, heating her, nearly setting her on fire.

When he finally broke the kiss, she was breathing hard, and he laughed. "Thought it was just me."

"Nope," she said, touching her mouth. "Definitely not just you."

He wrapped an arm around her shoulders. "Come on. Let's get inside before we freeze to death."

She followed him into the barn, where it was surprisingly snug. There was the sharp smell of animals, the sound of them moving in the hay.

And then she looked over and saw Betsy in her stall. She was standing up, straw in her mane and tail. But she was standing. She had a tube in her nose, and Lucky's dad stood beside her, stroking her neck.

"Hello, Mr. Elliott," she said.

He glanced up, seeming at home in this barn. More comfortable than when he'd been all dressed up at the auction, surrounded by sparkling champagne and fancy people. She guessed this was his element.

"Hi, Rachel. Merry Christmas."

"I'm so sorry about Betsy," she said. "I thought I'd come out and keep Lucky company tonight."

Hank Elliott's gaze shifted to his son. "He's very fortunate to have someone care enough to come out here on Christmas Eve. And I'm grateful, too. Thank you."

Rachel looked at the donkey again and frowned. She did know enough about farm animals to realize it was a good sign she was on her feet. "How's she doing?"

Lucky kept his hand on her lower back, and she loved how it felt there. Like it belonged. "Her fever is down a little. I think she's responding to treatment. We hope, at least."

Giving the donkey a pat, Hank pulled the tube gently out of her nose. She shook her head as he rubbed her withers and said something to her they couldn't hear. Then he stepped away and opened the stall door. "She should be good for a while. I'm going to go inside and leave you kids to it. Let me know if she takes a turn, Lucky. Otherwise, I'll be back in an hour or so."

"Okay, Dad."

"I'm sure your grandmother will be out soon with some sort of baked goods. Or warm cider. Or both." He walked by and gave Rachel a tired smile. "Hope you brought your appetite."

She smiled back and watched him head out into the snowy night, toward the house and all its comfort and joy.

Lucky took her hand and pulled her close. "I think he likes you."

"I like him. He reminds me of you."

He gazed down at her with those eyes that were the color of worn blue jeans. Or the lake on a cloudy day. He was so handsome, for a second, all she could do was stare.

"I think we're more alike than I ever thought," he said. "It wasn't until tonight that I really saw it."

She grazed her bottom lip with her teeth, tasting her lip gloss. Tasting him. "Did you tell your family about the offer on the farm?"

"I did. And I don't think they want to sell. Maybe in the future we'll get to the point where we need to let go of some acreage to keep the place going, and that's okay. But we'll cross that bridge when we come to it."

She smiled slowly. "Does this mean…"

"The sanctuary? Probably. I mean, I've got no other excuses, right?"

He winked. That signature Lucky wink that she'd come to love.

"It's what I want," he continued. "Deep down."

She opened her mouth to tell him how proud she was, but he put a finger to her lips before she could say anything.

"But that's not what I wanted to talk to you about," he said.

The barn was quiet, peaceful. Betsy stood in her stall with her eyes half-closed. She was dozing. Comfortable.

The two donkeys were separated by their stalls, but were standing as close as they could get to each other. Physically, spiritually in tune. It was maybe the sweetest thing Rachel had ever seen. And she'd once seen a dog nurse a litter of kittens.

"The sanctuary is great," Lucky said. "The fact that Patrick wants to go in on it with me, that you believe in it like you do…those things are great. But it's not what I've been thinking about these last few days. It's not what I couldn't get out of my head, no matter how hard I tried."

She slid her arms underneath his jacket and around his waist. He was lean and hard. Everything she'd thought a cowboy would be up close. But Lucky was no ordinary cowboy. He was the toughest man, with the biggest heart, she'd ever met in her life.

"What couldn't you get out of your head?" she asked, pressing herself against him.

"You," he said simply.

She gazed up at him, loving the moment for everything it was. Seeing in him someone who'd come full circle. Someone who'd been afraid of dreaming, but was now giving himself permission to do just that.

"You're the reason I want to stay in Marietta," he said. "When it came right down to it, I don't think I could've left."

"Maybe I would've followed you," she said, hooking her thumbs in his belt loops. "Wherever you decided to go."

He leaned down close, breathing warmth against her lips, and defying all the rules of the frigid winter night. Somewhere above them, above the steely clouds and falling snow of Christmas Eve, the north star glittered over the barn. Over Montana herself.

"Hey," he said quietly, almost kissing her. But not quite yet. Making her wait. And teaching her how many things in life were worth waiting for.

"What?"

"I've got a great first kiss story for you…"

She grinned, feeling her heart expand inside her chest. It filled her up. Made her whole where she'd been broken before.

And he pressed his lips to hers.

Epilogue

LUCKY PULLED ON the long leather reins, easing Dreamer to a stop alongside the curb. The little horse shook his head, the bells attached to his harness jingling in the warm night air.

This was only his third time pulling the two-seater antique carriage, and Lucky couldn't have been prouder. Dreamer had taken to it quickly, and the work had turned out to be good for him. He was a horse that needed to be stimulated, exercised regularly, to be his happiest. And he looked beautiful pulling the carriage—regal and dark in front of the bright red paintjob, with the names of the sanctuary and farm emblazoned on the side. *Christmas Eve Animal Sanctuary, at Sleigh Bell Farm, Marietta, Montana.*

Tonight, the heavy snows of December were just a distant memory. The July night was unusually warm for Montana, and stars sparkled overhead, crowding the heavens. Soon, the fireworks would start, and he had the perfect place to take Rachel to watch them—on the grassy bluff above the fairgrounds. Normally, he'd be working late on the fourth of July, catering to families and young couples who wanted to take a ride on a balmy summer evening. But, tonight, he and

Dreamer had closed shop early. They had something to celebrate, and he'd wanted to do it right.

He looked up at Rachel's apartment window and the sheer, white curtains billowing in the breeze. She'd recently hit her stride with the podcast, drawing the attention of several national sponsors. It had even been listed as a *Best Listen* by a popular morning talk show, catapulting her into near stardom. Or, at least, as far as she was concerned.

She had people lining up to tell their first kiss stories, and she'd finally been able to give her notice at the Graff last week. She'd really miss it, but this was her biggest dream come true, and they'd thrown her a farewell party fit for a podcasting princess. Lucky had come. So had his grandparents, and her mom. Chloe and Bob. Everyone who loved her had been there. Watching her glow from the inside out. She'd been radiant. And she was his.

Tonight, he wanted to finish what they'd started all those months ago. When they'd been headed to dinner to have that drink—to toast the podcast, to toast the sanctuary. And to celebrate the beginning of something that neither one of them could've realized would turn into something as precious as it had.

Behind the carriage seat, there was a blanket and some chilled wine. Some cheese and crackers, and some chocolates, Rachel's favorites from Copper Mountain Chocolate Shop. Nothing fancy. But they weren't a fancy couple. Their favorite time together was often spent just like this—on carriage rides through town, when Pete took a rare night off. On quiet horseback rides across the farm or on drives to interview couples for future podcast episodes.

Rachel wasn't just Lucky's lover now. She was his best friend. His partner and, together with Patrick, the one he trusted most to give him guidance on the sanctuary. It was a wild, sometimes complicated, but always heartfelt adventure that he'd embarked on. He didn't know where he'd be without her. Not nearly as settled. And definitely not as happy.

The door to her apartment opened, and she stepped out holding a small bundle in her arms. She smiled and waved before locking the door and heading down the steps toward the street.

"Hey, baby," she said. She had a slight sunburn from yesterday—her cheeks were pink and freckled underneath the light of the streetlamp. She'd come out to help with Dave and Betsy's new turnout on the side of the barn— something he'd built so they'd have more room to be together, with plenty of shade on summer's hottest days. Betsy had recovered beautifully, and he'd been spoiling her rotten, not taking any chances on a relapse.

Rachel gave Dreamer a pat as she walked around to the other side of the carriage and climbed up, still clutching the bundle. She wore a white sundress with a denim jacket. Her dark hair was soft and loose around her face, and she smiled as she settled on the seat beside him.

He leaned in to kiss her. She tasted like honey. "Hey, gorgeous," he said, pulling away to look down at the blanket in her arms. "Uh…I'm afraid to ask."

Her grin widened, and she looked like a teenager then.

She got this way around animals. It was in her blood, too.

"I had a listener call this morning," she said. "She found him in a drainage ditch behind Monroe's Market. He was all alone, no siblings. Maybe something got to his mother?"

He reached down and pulled the blanket open. There, nestled in its folds, was a fuzzy yellow duckling. He blinked up at Lucky with little button eyes and quacked. He looked perfectly content in Rachel's arms. But, then again, who wouldn't be?

"Poor thing," he said. "Has he had anything to drink?"

"Some water. And he seems healthy for the most part. Scared at first, but he let us pick him right up. I was afraid to leave him here tonight—he'd end up being a Lucy snack."

Lucky smiled, tucking the blanket around the duckling again. "Good idea."

"Do you think there's room at the sanctuary?" Rachel asked, her eyes big. "I know large animals are your specialty, but I'll come out and take care of him myself…"

"There's always room. That's our motto, remember? And if, eventually we don't have room, we'll find a place that does."

Sitting back against the seat, she gazed at him, her long, dark lashes casting shadows over her cheeks. "I'm glad I know you, Lucky Elliott. You know that?"

"I'm glad I know you too. Wait…scratch that. I'm glad I'm sleeping with you."

She laughed, and it rang like a bell through the warm night air.

A firecracker popped in the sky, followed by another and

another. They bloomed into kaleidoscopes of reds, whites, and blues, lighting up the darkness, filling it with color.

And that's what Rachel had done to his world. She'd lit it up. She'd set it on fire. It was unlike any fire that he'd ever known—and it burned with love and hope.

"I think we're too late for the fireworks on the hill," she said, reaching for his hand and pulling it into her lap where the duckling slept.

He leaned over and pushed her hair back behind her ear. Then kissed her cheek. Dreamer nickered softly, jingling the bells on his harness. For the first time in a very long time, Lucky felt like he was finally home.

"It's okay," he said against her skin. "We've got plenty right here."

The End

If you enjoyed this book, please leave a review at your favorite online retailer! Even if it's just a sentence or two it makes all the difference.

Thanks for reading *Christmas at Sleigh Bell Farm* by Kaylie Newell!

Discover your next romance at TulePublishing.com.

TULE
PUBLISHING

If you enjoyed *Christmas at Sleigh Bell Farm,*
you'll love the next book in….

The Elliotts of Montana series

Book 1: *Christmas at Sleigh Bell Farm*

Book 2: *Coming in April 2020!*

Available now at your favorite online retailer!

More books by Kaylie Newell

The Harlow Brothers series

The Harlow brothers learned at a young age that family is what you make of it. Born on the wrong side of the tracks and abandoned by their father, Judd, Luke and Tanner have grown into remarkably tough men who are jaded by life. But when they come together as guardians of their orphaned half-sister, they'll find that love is what you make of it, too. As they learn how to be the fathers they never had, their carefully constructed walls begin to crack. But it will take three strong women to tear those defenses down for good, and show them what true happiness looks like.

Book 1: *Tanner's Promise*

Book 2: *Luke's Gift*

Book 3: *Judd's Vow*

Available now at your favorite online retailer!

If you enjoyed *Christmas at Sleigh Bell Farm*,
you'll love these other Tule Christmas books!

Claiming the Cowboy for Christmas
by Kadie Scott

Christmas with the Firefighter
by Clare Connelly

A Texas Christmas Wish
by Alissa Callen

Available now at your favorite online retailer!

About the Author

For Kaylie Newell, storytelling is in the blood. Growing up the daughter of two gifted writers, she knew eventually she'd want to follow in their footsteps. While she's written short stories her whole life, it wasn't until after her kids were born that she decided to shoot for the moon and write her first romance novel. She hasn't looked back since!

Kaylie lives in Southern Oregon with her husband, two little girls, two indifferent cats and a mutt named Pedro.

Thank you for reading

Christmas at Sleigh Bell Farm

If you enjoyed this book, you can find more from all our great authors at TulePublishing.com, or from your favorite online retailer.

TULE
PUBLISHING

CPSIA information can be obtained
at www.ICGtesting.com
Printed in the USA
LVHW100815271222
735909LV00032B/439